CW00866656

IMAGINED
REALITIES

Collection of Short Stories and Poetry

By

John K. Geraghty

Dedicated to:

*Ross Scrivener – my best friend and carer, who has
sacrificed so much for me.*

Michael Geraghty – my brother.

*Cathy Holgate – my dear friend, who submitted the
manuscript and worked so hard arranging this.*

Gillian George for the illustrations.

CONTENTS

1

Miss Margery Montrose Bone...

My first encounter with Miss Bone was on a cold, damp autumn evening. There was drizzle in the air and as I left home in the darkening gloom I was having second thoughts... Why had I agreed to go? My initial excitement had already evaporated... 10

pence an hour no longer seemed so inviting... and yet the sweets I could buy with 20 pence or even 30 pence spurred me on. My green and black bicycle with its yellow mudguards moved swiftly past the Heath and into the alley behind the Jolly Sailor pub. It was always a relief when you came out the other end... it stank of stale urine and beer... and had a sinister silence that unnerved me.

At the top of Harpenden Road stood a row of impressive-looking Victorian houses... three floors and attics that were not strictly attics... more like passageways in between inner and outer walls, but more of that later... Miss Margery Montrose Bone lived in the first house after a pair of houses with an open drive. As I reached her gate I had little comprehension of the 'world' I was about to enter. The gate was shrouded in dripping, decaying trees... shedding their leaves... creating a slippery carpet on the broken, greasy steps up to the path that led to the back door. I lifted my bike up these steps then went down to push the broken and rotten gate to. As I did so, woodlice skittered across my hands and up my arms. I brushed them away, along with the mildew... green and wet. In my panic to get up the steps again, I slipped and scraped my face on an overgrown bush... blood leaked from my cheek.

Finally I reached the door and knocked... there was a bell but it was broken. There was no answer so I called out and knocked again. Suddenly a window was thrust open above me and what met my eyes was the face of nightmares!

I wanted to flee but I could not move... she stared down at me in all her wild glory and hissed, 'Who are you?' I stumbled backwards... broken glass crunching beneath my feet...

There at the window was the most extraordinary vision... even looking up to the landing window I could see how dirty and dishevelled she was... the skin on her face was like a cracked riverbed that had been violently hit by a sharp thunderstorm. Her lips were thin and bloodless, around her mouth were the remains of some vile meal... Her small, searching eyes – a washed-out blue – took in the small, shaking boy below. She opened her mouth to speak again and bits of rancid food fluttered down onto my upturned face...

'I am John,' I stammered...

'You are a very dirty boy... as far as I can see. What is all that muck on your arms and face? Have you been fighting? I don't want a violent, dirty boy working for me, and you are rather small!'

I was close to shouting up, 'You cheeky, old witch... who are you calling dirty? What about you?!' But I held my tongue, as she threw down a set of rusty keys and told me to come up so she could inspect me... and with that she slammed the window shut. I waited a moment then selected a key... it turned in the lock and I shoved the door open. The smell of decay was appalling and I retched at the sight of a dead mouse on the stairs up to the first floor. As I neared the top of the stairs, an even more disgusting smell hit my nostrils...

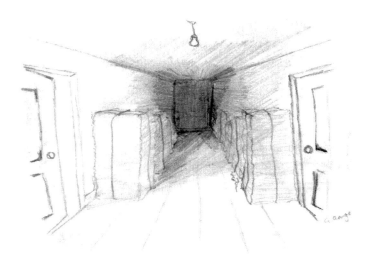

I could feel bile burning in my throat and my eyes were starting to smart and blur. At the top of the stairs, directly ahead, lay a passageway, lined on either side with tall bundles of newspapers tied with string... It was too dark too see what lay further down in this direction but the awful smell was coming from there... but there was another smell... strong and powerful...TCP! To my left there was a dim light shining into the space where I stood...

Across from this was a closed door and to the right of that sat a filthy Baby Belling cooker. I moved towards the light and a half-open door... She must be in there... no other lights were on... Indeed, that was where she was... in all her splendid awfulness. She was sitting in a threadbare chair... a small table was resting against her spindly legs that were swathed in surgical stockings. The table was laden with all manner of things... bottles of TCP, packets of tea, jars of honey, mouldy slices of bread, a bread knife, and an uncut brown loaf. There were scraps of food all around her – on the floor, sideboard, even in her chair.

She was so painfully thin, and yet there was a whole grocery store in this room... tins mainly... but jars of baby food too... the whole range of flavours!

'So boy... come closer, I won't bite you! You really are smaller than I imagined,' she hissed...

I started to back away, for fear of vomiting. It was the first time I had seen her teeth... the darkest of yellow and encrusted in a thick film of greyish mucus that seemed to shift and dribble onto her chin as she spoke again. 'Your duties, boy, will be many and varied. I will try you out for a few weeks to see if you suit. Sundays at 10.00... That will be when you come... You still have the keys. I will have them back if you please!'

I moved gingerly forward and placed them into her grubby hand... and as I did so, I was startled by the bulging veins in her paper-thin wrist. The hand was lightning fast as it closed over the keys.

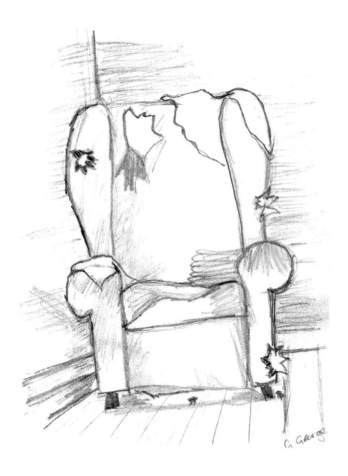

'And now, boy, sit... I will list your duties... There! Over there boy... Shift those papers and clothes, and be careful with them... Now sit!'

I did as I was told, though before I sat down I quickly wiped my hands on the side of the chair. The papers were soiled and the clothes damp... both had the odour of urine. I was about 10 feet from her when she shifted in her chair and then rose to her feet and moved towards the fireplace... and then towards me... I was terrified... but then she stopped dead, swivelled like a crane, and returned to her seat... I sighed and my racing heart slowed... I waited...

'Are you about to listen, boy? Your duties will include coal, cinders, milk bottles, shopping, gardening, lighting fires, sorting newspapers, sweeping...' She took a deep breath then continued, 'Cleaning, messages, staying overnight, when required, cutting my toenails, soaking my feet, and anything else I ask you to do. Do you understand?'

I was speechless... What?! All this for 10p an hour!

At this point she seemed to tire and close her eyes... I stood up and instantly she was awake, her eyes sharp and darting... 'Well... let me show you round... obviously this is the room where I live but there are many rooms, mostly unlocked...'

She then put her slippers on, covering her gnarled feet and misshapen toes... She was now shuffling towards me and was soon by my side...

'Come, boy...' And with that she took my arm and firmly propelled me through the door and across the landing into the dining room... It was spacious but cluttered... there was not the chaos of the room she lived in...

The smell in here was of mustard... in all the time I worked for her I never understood or discovered why... Other smells in the house all had an explanation. In this room I was to 'sleep' one winter, when she wasn't well. Three nights of terror, unexplained noises, voices, and 'apparitions'.

We then moved swiftly into the next two rooms... empty but for the tottering bundles of newspapers. Next she steered me down the passageway to the bathroom and toilet, both full of thick cobwebs and dust, then right, into the kitchen... Here there was a long wooden table, mostly obscured by unwashed milk bottles... the smell was overpowering. Some were just grubby, but most had the remnants of milk in them... curdled sludge of various colours!

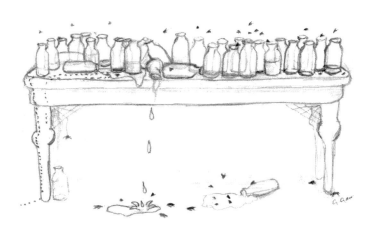

Some were very old, maybe years old; the sludge had grown hard and black.

It was in this room that the colonies of spiders, cockroaches, and ants had chosen to reside... though not exclusively!

Then we were back up the unlit passageway... She stopped at the top of the stairs and looked up...

'Second floor and attic rooms.' She made no move to go up... she was intent on going down to the ground floor, which disappointed me because the aroma, faint but distinct, was of fermenting apples... explained later when I saw the ancient orchard at the top of the garden, beyond the former tennis lawn.

She let go of my arm and unclenched her hand, passing the keys into mine.

'Downstairs is an empty flat and outside is the garden and the sheds... When you come on Sunday I will show you... but now it is dark and you must go... Lock up and put the keys through the letterbox... Don't be late on Sunday.'

And with that I was dismissed and given a surprisingly rough shove... She turned her back on me and shuffled off. A light went on as I reached the bottom of the stairs... an outside light which illuminated my way to the door. Briefly, I thought about the downstairs flat... but all I wanted was to get out. Once outside and with the door locked, I pushed the keys through and the light snapped off... I couldn't see a thing but felt my bike at my feet, picked it up and wheeled it down the slippery path to the steps and gate. The street lights were on and the fine drizzle had become rain as I pedalled away.

*

Sunday morning came... and my second visit loomed... It was cold and foggy... the rain the previous night had left the paths greasy and covered in an extra carpet of leaves... I was tired and irritable.

My journey to Miss Bone's was uneventful, not so my arrival! As I wheeled my bike up to the back door, the window snapped open and the keys were flung down with such force that they bounced straight up and hit me in the lip and then fell into one of the innumerable coal boxes that stretched from the back door, and off onto the cinder path that ran along the rear of the house... I scooped the keys up... and felt blood trickling down my chin. I opened the door and there was a list on a grubby piece of torn paper, on the hall floor: *Coal, Floors, Stairs, Fires, Newspapers.*

I called up but there was no response... so I turned and went back out and down the cinder path to the coal sheds. They were padlocked but there were keys in my bunch to open them... Inside there were all manner of boxes to put coal in so, I began filling them. After about 20 minutes, I went back round to the door, pushed it open, and went in. I climbed the stairs and started shifting the boxes and scuttles up the steps. At the top, I moved the ones on the landing close to the entrance to 'her room' and then worked my backwards and forwards, down the stairs... out onto the stone and then cinder path, until I reached the sheds. The continuous line of coal now stretched, unbroken, from sheds to room... I had anticipated that a few extra boxes would be demanded so I had these in reserve... true enough, she demanded them... and seemed disappointed when I produced them.

'Floors now, boy… then the fires downstairs in the empty flat… then newspapers.' She threw a pack of fire-lighters at me and a ball of string, then pointed to a bucket with a smelly old towel in it and said, 'Fill that in the kitchen… I will meanwhile check there are no breaks in the line of coal.'

I set off for the kitchen and she proceeded with her inspection of the coal line… peering down the stairs and out through the windows overlooking the line. I reached the kitchen, and as I pushed at the door, something rushed out and past me. I jumped back, and fell into a huge dresser…

It was a bloody mouse! It skittered away up the passage, without a backward glance, and was gone. I pulled myself to my feet. My shoulder was sore and my heart was racing as I pushed the door further open... nothing else there but the appalling smell. I picked up the bucket and went into the kitchen. I turned on the rusty tap... it was stiff... but water came sputtering, gurgling out. The pipes groaned and shuddered as I filled the bucket... That done, I put it down and made a start on the disgusting milk bottles. The other tap – the hot water one – was green with age and completely disabled... The cold water was gushing now, into the Belfast sink... reddish brown.

I collected a selection of bottles and immersed them in the freezing water, switched off the tap, and looked round for something to clean them with. Under the sink I found an assortment of old rags, in various stages of decay. They reeked of fish but at least I could use them to wipe away the sludge coming out of the bottles... The sink was filled many times and I was beginning to feel I was getting somewhere. The time passed and I managed at least 50 bottles... it was enough. I drained the sink and pushed the remaining sediment down the plug hole, leaving the bottles upturned to dry.

I then picked up the bucket and made my way out to the dresser... I had spied some cleaner rags and some liquid floor polish when I had stumbled earlier. I grabbed both, and saw a broom too. I was now armed to tackle the stairs. I also assembled newspapers, the fire-lighters, and matches... I took these items down first and unlocked the flat... I put them inside... I went back up and started on the stairs, leaving the liquid polish and rags on the top step. The sweeping was soon done and I left the broom inside the downstairs flat. I then wiped the stairs clean and left them to dry.

The hallway, downstairs, was relatively easy; I worked my way from the back door to the flat door, left the bucket there and went in, carrying my fire-lighting equipment on top of a box of coal from the hall. (All the boxes I had moved and put back whilst cleaning the floor... the box I had was replaced by another on the stairs... but there was now a gap in the line, so I had to replace that with one of those I had hidden in the shrubs by the back door! As ever, I never thought logically and it took me a few weeks to work out a system.)

The fires were duly lit and the floor and stairs now dry... so I then started the whole process again... moving boxes, applying polish... trying to buff with the dry rags... remember the boxes lined hall and stairs on both sides... It took ages but was finally done. All the equipment then went into the now empty bucket and back up the stairs I went. Four hours had passed and I was really tired. My shoulder ached and my fat lip burned.

She was waiting for me on the landing with a grime-smeared cup of cold tea and a mouldy water biscuit... 'It is fine China tea... sit, boy... You have done three hours... so here is the 30p.' I didn't move... It was four hours!

I found my voice... I was angry. 'Miss Bone... it was four hours,' I stammered. There was silence but she could see I was not going to budge and her grubby hand scooped out another 10p from her battered, capacious bag... and then she smiled. 'Drink up... you must go now... check the fires before you leave, lock up, and put the keys through the door.'

Once I was outside, the window was flung open

and she watched me go, shouting after me, 'Next Sunday at 10.00... Don't be late!'

My first Sunday was over. It was the calm before the storm. Sundays would be interspersed with Saturdays and Wednesdays... and the horrors of those days were yet to come...

The call came late on Wednesday afternoon... it was her... all I heard were the final few words of the conversation. 'Yes I see, yes I will tell him.'

Apparently prescriptions, purified water, and beef tea were to be collected from the chemists. The money would be left outside and I was to go straight there. 'You can have your tea when you get back... you'd better get going now... sooner there, sooner back.' And so my first Wednesday visit ensued. It was already dusk when I set off... the street lamps already on... I pedalled as fast as I could, shot down the alley behind the pub, rounded the corner and was there... I left my bike outside the gate and ran to the back door. On the path was a small leather purse with a metal clip and the keys... both were shoved into my pocket and I was off into town.

Boots was ablaze with lights as I pushed open the doors... All the items to be collected were waiting for me. The girl behind the counter smirked. 'You must be Miss Bone's boy!' I nodded... handed over the money from the purse... grabbed the items and skidded on the wet floor! The girl stifled her guffaws... and I was up and gone... but not before I heard her tinkling laughter as the doors swung shut. I rested the water on one arm of the handlebars and stuffed the other items in my coat pocket, along with the horrid little purse...

I was soon back at the house... I opened the door and went in... It was pitch black and I had to feel my way upstairs. On the landing, the light was on and the lights to the upper floor...? I was puzzled. Suddenly she was there!

'Before you go... take a look upstairs... You will be up there on Sunday... to sort the apples...'

Was she leering at me? Had she noticed the terror in my eyes? Before I made my way up, she handed me 10p and I passed over her purchases and the purse...

Upstairs the bare bulb shone into a gloomy bedroom. This was where the apples were... but they were not alone... she heard me gasp and let out a cry of disbelief. The upper room was infested with cockroaches, feasting on the putrid apples... I slammed the door shut and galloped down the stairs. When I reached the landing she was cackling! 'Till next Sunday then... off you skedaddle... keys through the letterbox...'

I didn't say goodbye... I just fled.

When I reached the alley... I hesitated... My fear of dark places was to be well-founded that night and on subsequent nights. As I raced into the bowels of the alley something caught in the spokes of my bike and I was pitched forward...

The bike hit the pub back wall and I tumbled into the path of a big, fat, menacing boy...

'I've been waiting for you...' he snarled. The stale sweat was pouring off him as he reached down and dragged me to my feet...

The boy pushed me roughly against the wall, grabbed my throat and rifled through my pockets. His fingers pinched my skin as he did so... He found the 10p in a flash and his triumphant, piercing whoop was accompanied by a huge gob of spit, green and glutinous, that planted itself firmly in my hair. He then pocketed the 10p and with his now free hand, smeared and rubbed the gob of spit into my scalp. Swiftly, he then kicked my legs from under me and as I fell he landed on top of my chest and pinned my arms down... His face was close to mine when coughed up more 'phlegm', opened his mouth and let it dribble into both my eyes... I struggled to avoid it, but he forced up one of my arms and whacked it heavily into my chin... My mouth opened involuntarily and more spit was produced with alarming speed...

'Swallow it... you little bastard,' he hissed. His knees were now holding down my arms and his pudgy fingers were pushing into my throat... I swallowed and was promptly sick... all over his trousers! With that he punched me really hard in the ear, and scraped the sick from his trousers and deposited it on my face.

He then stood up slowly, glared at me, kicked my bike and ran off into the darkness... I picked myself up and pedalled home... On the way I was sick once more and I could feel blood oozing from my swollen ear. My clothes were dirty, my jacket torn, and my face burned with shame and drying vomit...

Sunday came around all too quick... the memory of the previous Wednesday evening persuaded me to take a different route to Miss Bone's house. It was sunny as I set off... I went across the Heath... through the woods and up the Harpenden Road. I arrived at 10.00 on the dot but by that time there were angry clouds above and a storm was brewing. The keys were by the back door... I opened it quickly, pushed my bike into the hall and locked up behind me. I wasn't quite sure whether my assailant knew where I had been or where I was going to... but I was now nervous on two counts... the 'apple room' and him. When I got to the top of the stairs, Miss Bone was there... she handed me my list... Coal, then upstairs. The coal was easily sorted... I cheated. I had hidden three boxes in the downstairs flat, so went down to get them and swapped them with three in the hall... I waited a bit before I went back up.

She had already returned to her room and was eating her breakfast of cereal and grapefruit as I put the boxes by the door... She was a noisy eater and she did not look up when I told her I was going up. So far she had spoken very little to me and this morning she had said nothing. I switched on the light and made my way up.

The door to the 'apple room' was open and though my heart was pumping, I thought I knew what to expect... It was unchanged... and yet it was different. The rotten apples were still writhing under the onslaught of the cockroaches as I set about gingerly removing the worst of them. I wrapped these in loose newspaper... and must have spent at least an hour rearranging the rest. Then I set about the piles of untied newspapers... just stacking them and making them neat... It was whilst I was doing this that I noticed the wardrobe at the back of the room and the doorway to the left of it. Why hadn't I noticed either on the Wednesday? I stopped what I was doing and crossed the room...

I was feeling quite light-headed from the decaying apples but I was intrigued by what turned out to be two locked doors. I had the bunch of keys and sure enough, both doors opened. The wardrobe was capacious but very old and dirty. Inside there were big, heavy, fur coats... covered in cobwebs. I chose not to climb in that day but instead turned my attention to the other door I had unlocked. I turned the handle slowly and edged the door open... inside was a long, thin passageway, but before I even entered I was overwhelmed by hundreds of enormous spiders... Suffice to say I slammed the door shut, frantically brushing off as many spiders as I could. I locked the door and then the wardrobe door. There were still spiders crawling all over me as I left the room and headed smartly downstairs.

Miss Bone had finished her breakfast and was waiting for me as I entered the room... 20p was sitting on the table in front of her. 'There, boy... your money... It is time for you to go... not been stealing up there... have you?' She grabbed my wrist really tightly and hung on...

'No... Of course I haven't!' I was incensed she could even have thought it, though coins and notes were spread generously all over that first floor of the house and I soon found myself handing them over at regular intervals on subsequent visits.

She let go of my wrist and shocked me by patting my arm and saying brightly, 'You have done well today... you did lock those two doors, didn't you?'

What?! How did she know?!

At that, she buried her face in the remains of a grapefruit and rubbed vigorously, whilst muttering, 'Good for the skin...' I had escaped the tea and biscuits and was soon out of there... posting the keys as usual. The 20p was safely in my sock as I made my way home the way I had come... The thunder and lightning and the pelting rain comforted me. There was no sign of my attacker and going this way meant, that if I did chance upon him, I could dodge him on the open Heath. Over lunch I did muse briefly about Miss Bone knowing I had opened those two doors... How could she know? Unless she had crept up the stairs and been watching me!

*

Over the next few weeks I went to Miss Bone's and slowly got used to her strange ways and barking commands, but during that time the two doors upstairs – the wardrobe and the attic doors – were firmly locked... the keys to both were mysteriously missing from the bunch. She never mentioned them and I never asked. Autumn quickly turned into winter and one Sunday in mid-December I woke to find thick snow on the ground. It meant I would have to walk there and worse still, walk back. At first it was exciting, trudging through the crisp snow, but I soon grew cold... It seemed to take ages to get there and I was constantly worrying that I might meet the boy from the alley... I had not seen him for ages and yet I instinctively knew he was still about.

Upon arrival, the trees were dripping with icicles and the snow on the path showed all the tell-tale signs of rats... Tiny footprints... right up to the back door! I knew they were resident in the garden but today this concrete evidence made me nervous. The keys were on the ground, as usual, and I unlocked and went in. The house was quiet and there was no instructions note on the floor. I climbed the stairs, a little puzzled... There was nothing to suggest anyone was there... and when I reached her room, it was empty.

'Is that you... boy? Come through, I am in the dining room.' I then heard her coughing. Immediately I entered I realised she was sick. She lay on the large sofa, swathed in blankets up to her neck and sporting an extraordinary wool bonnet! She beckoned me to come forward and rasped, 'Just upstairs today... just upstairs,' and then she waved me away.

As I fiddled with the keys on my way up I noticed the two missing keys were now back on the ring! I fairly jumped up the stairs and hurried into the room. Unlocking the attic door was like being given an unexpected present... The spiders flooded out and I smartly stepped aside... I could see inside. Right by the door were some very old books... and... a torch! It was definitely not there before... I switched it on and then moved warily through the doorway and on... About ten feet in the door slammed violently shut and I screamed and dropped the torch...

My initial panic was followed by anger... I flicked at whatever it was probing my ear and crouched down to feel about for the torch... I soon located it but in its fall the batteries had dislodged. I knew I was not far from the door, so crawled towards it, feeling my way in the dark. I reached out for the bookcase opposite the door... bingo... I was there. Covered in cobwebs, I stood, turned, and leaned forward... the door! I felt down for the handle, whilst pushing on the door. It seemed stuck but was definitely moving... With a final shove it gave way and I tumbled out into the light. Relief washed over me.

Composing myself, I faced the door again. If there had been anyone in the room, they were gone now. I wedged a stack of newspapers against the door and went back in. I found the batteries almost immediately and reassembled the torch. The bookcase was full of ancient journals... I randomly selected a couple and brought them back into the room and sat down on the floor, ignoring the mouse droppings and the spiders. I carefully opened the first of the dusty books and my eyes widened as I beheld the glorious, yellowing, sepia photographs. There were so many but it was clear they were of the house and gardens long ago. The second book contained photographs of Miss Bone and her family... it was a revelation. The crabby old woman downstairs was once a beauty! Inscriptions below each photograph confirmed who everyone was... and right at the back was a family tree.

I put the books aside and steeled myself to go back inside the attic room... This time I made sure the door was securely propped open, and for good measure pushed some single newspapers into the gap between the door and its frame. I tried to push it shut but it held firm... so in I went. At the entrance I shone the torch into the darkness. It was like no other attic I had ever seen. It was long and narrow, with shelves all along one side. I ventured further in... Curiously, I was now unafraid. The chuckling I had heard earlier outside the door, I put down to imagination and fear.

Towards the far end of this 'passage' the torch lit on three large portraits... As the light danced over them I was sure the eyes were moving... trick of the light... and yet... A noise at the door, now behind me, caused me to stiffen; I abandoned any thought of further investigation and ran for the door... It was already shifting when I reached it. There was no one in the room when I emerged but back in the attic I distinctly heard that sinister chuckling again! I unstopped the door, pushed it shut and locked it. The wardrobe could wait for another day! As I left the room a mouse appeared and then another! Enough... I was away down the stairs pretty sharpish and back into the dining room. Seemingly she hadn't moved.

'So, had enough? Mmm... you have certainly been a busy little boy! There's your money... it is snowing quite hard outside and you do not have your bike... so off you trot.' She sighed and then said, rather ominously, 'I will give your mother a call, if I am no better in a couple of days...'

She was right, the snow was falling heavily as I locked the door and thrust the keys inside and bolted down the path... my 20p safely in my sock, or so I thought. I decided to take the alleyway home... it was quicker and it wasn't dark. Big mistake... it turned out to be my second encounter with the bully, who had terrified me and invaded my dreams for weeks. This time I did not get off so lightly...

I entered the alley with trepidation but the snow was worrying me, swirling in the strengthening wind... I had to get home as quickly as I could... A few yards into the alley I thought of going back out onto the road... I could see nothing behind me and nothing before me... I hesitated just too long before I made my decision and a voice penetrated the silent blizzard... menacing and familiar, despite the fact that I had only ever heard it once before...

'Hellow there... Long time no see, you little bastard...'

Fear, panic, and revulsion descended. Just as he grabbed me I tore free and bolted forward... Running for my life, I disappeared into the snowy mist. I was running blind but he was right on my tail; I could hear him panting and wheezing. I knew he was close but I thought I could outrun him. But running blind I had not accounted for the brick wall behind the pub and as I hit it I bounced off and sprawled on the deepening snow... I tried to rise but was sent flying as he rammed into me.

Instantly he was upon me like a wild animal, pinning me down as before. I was powerless. His sour breath washed over me and my throat constricted.

'Got you, shit face... you're gonna pay for running away.' He sniggered. I almost laughed at this thuggish 'poet'... almost... but my concern was that I would piss my pants. He quickly searched my pockets but found nothing and then shifted his fat body round so his knees were still on my arms; he then proceeded to take my shoes and socks off... He grunted with satisfaction when he found the 20p. He pocketed it and shifted round again. From his other pocket he removed a matchbox and placed it on the ground, near my neck... then slid it slyly open... Oh my god! Earwigs! Gently, almost lovingly, he teased them out onto the cold snow... They raced for the warmth of my body. They were wriggling in my hair, probing my ears, and crawling under my shirt. I opened my mouth to scream and he thrust a handful of dirty snow, full of grit, straight down my throat. My nose and eyes were next... the grit stung and the snow smelt vaguely of piss. He couldn't do any more... could he? Well I am afraid he did...

He had come armed with a thin stick and there was shit on his shoes, which he delicately scraped off, and applied with sweeping strokes all over my face and clothes.

He stood slowly, smiled and helped me to my feet... only to kick my legs from under me...

'Till next time... eh?' And with that he vanished into the snow. I recovered my shoes and socks and then started to shake violently and burst into uncontrollable sobbing. I had been totally humiliated and was now glad of the blizzard that muffled my shame... as I trudged home.

True to her word, the call came from Miss Bone. The snow still lay thick on the ground and I had hoped for a few days off school but there was no chance of that... the buses were still running. It was Thursday that the dreaded phone call informed me, via Mum, that I would be required Friday through till Sunday. Apparently Miss Bone had been moved into the living room and I was to sleep in the dining room... I was to take Friday off and arrive at 12.00 when the private nurse left for the weekend. Thursday night was full of mixed emotions... on the one hand I still had the wardrobe to explore but the previous Sunday had left me traumatised. I woke early and spent the morning cleaning my bike, hoping I would be able to use it, but the roads were icy and the paths still impassable. I would have to go across the Heath and through the woods.

I set off about 11.00 and although it was very cold, the sun was shining... The journey was uneventful and I arrived just before 12.00. The keys were in the snow by the door and as I opened up, the nurse came bustling down. She informed me Miss Bone was asleep and my bed was made up... She would be back on Sunday... early. I was to keep the fire alight and also light the fires downstairs... I was to warm soup and make beef tea and serve the ready prepared food, what there was; it was to be warmed through on the baby cooker and left to cool. When required I was to feed Miss Bone and was told very sternly not to poke around... My normal duties were to be performed and there was a phone number to call if she worsened... The nurse stressed that Miss Bone was very sick and I was only to go into the room when called, or when the fire needed more coal. The nurse departed and I was left with the 'ailing' Miss Bone.

At first I busied myself with the fires downstairs, collected coal, washed milk bottles, and spent some time just wandering around the house and gardens... I was outside when it started snowing again... The orchard could wait... I was drawn to it but I couldn't say why. Once inside I rooted around the dining room, looking into books, whilst eating the jam sandwiches I had in my duffle bag. There were enough sandwiches, biscuits, and sweets for two days... a few cooking apples, two flasks of sweet tea and a bottle of diluted orange squash completed my 'stash'. Miss Bone slept on and darkness fell...

At about 7.00 she stirred and called me in, asking for food and beef tea. I had kept the baby food warm and just heated up the pan of tea... I took both in and fed her... she said nothing. I banked up the fire and went back to the dining room, climbed into bed and sat for a while reading one of the books I had picked up. I soon drifted off but was startled awake by the murmur of urgent voices. I jumped from the makeshift bed and looked in on her... she was snoring gently and had not moved. The mustard smell of the dining room was strong in the hall and when I stood at the bottom of the stairs to the upper floor I fancied I heard the murmuring voices growing into urgent whispers.

I listened for a short time but I couldn't make out what, if anything, was being said... I was imagining things. But back in the dining room I realised my bag had been moved... It was now over by the window and its contents had been spilled all over the floor... the smell of mustard was really strong. I repacked my bag and sat on the side of the bed. I started to shake... I was scared and cold. I didn't want to be there, but I was so tired and climbed into the bed and fell into a deep sleep.

When I woke, it was morning... sunlight streamed through the dirty windows and Miss Bone was calling me. As I clambered out of bed and put on my shoes I saw the five pound notes. Three of them scrunched up by the door! I picked them up and took them through to Miss Bone...she was sitting up eating grapefruit and demanding beef tea...she snatched the notes from me and clicked her teeth with her furry tongue. When I brought her tea in she was asleep once more...I added more coal to the embers of the fire and went out.

I was thirsty and hungry, so delved into my bag. After that I quickly looked in on her... She was definitely asleep... so I headed upstairs to the wardrobe and the albums. It was quiet and still up there... I collected the albums and climbed into the wardrobe and shut the door!

*

The wardrobe was warm and airless and entirely devoid of comfort... the fur coats therein were tatty and moth-eaten but the threadbare carpet on the floor shouted luxury and as I settled down the door creaked open and let in the natural light from the room... I opened both albums and immediately I heard the whispering voices, but this time they seemed friendly. The pictures seemed to come alive for me and after a while I closed my eyes and was transported far away to long ago, to a forgotten time when the house was young and the people in the photographs were vibrant and full of life and dreams... The whispering voices ceased their chatter and sighed contentedly as each page was turned and I closed my eyes, then opened them for the next. The whole morning passed in this fashion... and no word came from downstairs.

Nothing untoward happened all morning until the clock struck 12.00... then a piercing scream rang out. I scrambled out of the wardrobe and rushed downstairs.

Miss Bone lay on the floor in the hall... she was moaning, 'I called you, boy... why did you not come?' I managed to lift her emaciated frame and get her back into bed. I called the nurse... then put the beef tea on and warmed some food, but when I brought it in she was not there! I panicked... running from room to room... finally returning to the living room... and there she was... all cosy and fast asleep... food eaten, tea drunk!

The nurse arrived, irritable and looking at me with accusing eyes. I left the room and went outside to collect coal. After about half an hour she called me in and told me that I was to work for two more hours, then go home. A taxi would be calling for me and I should leave the keys with her... I worked out my shift... then waited in the hall for the taxi... As I was about to leave she thrust one of the crumpled fivers into my fist and put her finger to her lips. 'Miss Bone will see you next Sunday... don't be late!' As I left, I glanced up. I thought I saw Miss Bone and the nurse at the window! I was imagining it... I must be? The snow was thawing as I went down the path. The taxi was waiting... paid for, apparently, on Thursday evening, to collect on Saturday afternoon!

When I arrived at Miss Bone's the next Sunday, the albums and the wardrobe were gone... She was up and about and it was as if the previous weekend had never happened. Christmas was around the corner... but that is another story. The bully plagued me for a further three years... but those first few months with Miss Margery Montrose Bone were never again so eventful or shocking...

2

Going Home

Autumn was creeping in, the days growing shorter, the cold clear evenings washing the sky. It was May, soon to be June, and on one such evening Dicken Gathard prepared a snack. It was 11.30pm; a glass of milk mixed with hard chlorinated water, and a bumper cheese and salad cream butty. Dicken sat on the step and listened to the sleeping world – the dark night glorifying the peace – if only there were inner peace as well, mused Dicken. He was thirty-one, slightly overweight, and balding discernibly at the temples; he had felt slightly unwell, slightly unnerved for a measurable time, ever since his thirtieth birthday – in fact everything seemed slightly faded – even his career. He was a teacher in an African mission school – he had taught there when he was younger and had come back to recapture the sense of peace and wellbeing he had felt then. His return had only served to remind him that the peace of memory was not the peace of reality. He was going home to England soon, leaving for good – all the letters from home resounded with that phrase 'for good' – it made him feel slightly angry, heavy hearted and nauseous, but he knew it to be correct.

*

The cheese and salad cream tasted good, and the 'medicinal' drink ensured that the 'butty' would stay 'good' in his stomach – regular indigestion being a problem of late. This supper concoction varied in essence in only one aspect from normal Marmite and cheese, and was to have an extraordinary effect on his normal restless sleeping hours. In fact it would whip up a veritable frenzy.

The hand on the clock moved to twelve, and he wearily got up, closed the door and locked it. His last act before retiring to his lumpy bed was to switch the burglar alarm on and pull the curtains to. Once in bed he pulled the covers tightly around him and lay staring blankly at the rainwater stain on the ceiling. He was soon asleep – an uneventful sleep, that is until 2.30am, when woken by itching mosquito bites.

The clock in the living room struck the lonely half hour, and Dicken awoke – not in his bungalow bedroom in the interior of Africa, but on Nunn Avenue lined with the pink and white blossom he

knew so well as a child. He was dreaming, that was it...
and yet he knew he was no longer in 1990, but in 1971;
he was incredibly certain of this fact. Dicken Gathard,
nearly thirty-two, was in 1971, standing by the
telephone box, red and vandalised – that telephone
box was yellow now, and vandal proof, the letters from
home had told him so. A 391 bus sighed to a halt a
little further up the road and a gaggle of women
alighted, laden with Tesco shopping bags – plastic,
another sign that it certainly wasn't the nineties.

His heart began to beat a little faster – he knew all
of the women, fat, thin, embittered, sour, and jolly.
Mrs Turle, thin, and pinched Mrs Rose, gossipy Mrs
Adder and wicked, frail Mrs Spicer, and of course
limping Lou Hardacre; they all came towards him,
chattering. They all looked so fresh and alive – so
cheerful. If his memory served him well they would
all be gone with the exception of Mrs Rose, by 1988.
As they passed the telephone box they glanced up at
him and smiled – recognition, but not a word. He
watched them turn the corner into Marlen Grove, and
then his legs began to move him forward, in pursuit.
His gait was slow and difficult, and by the time he
reached the corner the women were gone.

He thought he should feel sad, but he wasn't, he
felt elated, just seeing them again. He passed the
woodyard, humming with activity, and crossed the
road. Number 2 Marlen Grove – the home of Mrs
Adder and her daughter – a daughter growing old,
ensnared by her grasping weasel of a mother, twisted
by her mother's emotional cruelty – but she would
finally escape with a secret love. Dicken knew this and
exulted in its certainty.

Number 4 Marlen Grove – the home of Mr and Mrs Field – not really Mr and Mrs; she was a lovely bird-like creature, silvery hair and perfectly fixed, gleaming white false teeth; he was her 'spouse' – today we use the term 'common law' – he cheated on her, but her ignorance was assured. She loved him and would never know where his bicycle took him.

Number 6 – The Turles. So delightful, so earthy, so real. He would die before her, but they were the perfect couple – even their fights were so good natured. Even as Dicken passed their gate he could feel their fire of kindness oozing through the blue pine door, with the highly polished knocker, and settling on the glorious beds of daffodils and tulips daffodils and tulips?! It was too late for such flowers, surely, thought Dicken.

Number 8 was next, and Dicken's toes tingled – Mrs Rose – already aged, but bound by time to travel well into her eighties, only to fail her century at the last hurdle. Mrs Rose and her yellow hedge and her hydrangea bushes, her fights with Mrs Turle, Mrs Welch, and Mrs Good, her wicked and wonderful tales of all inhabited Marlen Grove – infidelities, abortions, petty criminal acts – all known, and all stored – a microchip computer before its time.

Number 10 seemed to take a long time to reach, though only next door, and Dicken lingered over Number 8, remembering all the delicious scandal that lay therein, on the tip of that amazing tongue. But there was Number 10 – his home for 22 years, but for a spell at university. The gate worked – he never remembered it ever working! He lifted the latch and it swung smoothly open – the green of the garden struck him – neat and green, and then the brilliant red door and white step – a perfect purple clematis climbed an expertly nailed trellis to the right. Dicken was puzzled; true, a clematis had grown there, but the trellis had always been decidedly unstable. He stood before the door and felt impelled to knock; the blood coursed through his veins, bubbling in his brain, throbbing, hammering – warnings. He knocked. The door slowly opened and there, military style, was Uncle Frank. A look of recognition, a faint smile. Uncle Frank had lived at Number 10 ever since his wife Letty had died – he had departed in 1987. But this was 1971 – Uncle Frank stepped aside and gestured for Dicken to come in. Suddenly Dicken felt puffy, bloated.

The door closed behind him; Dicken could smell one of Uncle Frank's mouth-curling dinners on the stove, always accompanied by the pungent, disgusting smell of tripe and cabbage – that hadn't changed, Dicken thought. Dicken walked along the hall, past the front room – the door was open, and on the far side of the room Dicken saw the piano lid erect! Sheet music was neatly stacked on a small table to one side.

'Uncle Frank, who has been playing the piano?' Dicken was shocked – never had he seen the lid open, not since the time it came in the door in 1969 – it had been wheeled out, after his death, crumbling with disuse. It had never been used, the yellowing keys and the dust inside undisturbed.

'I have been playing, Dicken. These days I play quite a bit. Come into the back room, I've just made some tea.'

Dicken followed, he felt excited, but was tiring quickly. 'Mind the sausage dog, Dicken.' It was too late a warning, Dicken always tripped over the stupid door stopper. The room was as it should be, though despite it being May, for it must be with tulips and daffodils, there was a coal fire. As Dicken's eyes skirted the room he became aware that though superficially the same, it was in fact subtly different. The sideboard-cum-drink cabinet was open, and there was a full array of bottles, and clear-cut crystal glasses inside! Dicken only ever remembered one dusty, rather sickening bottle of 'Bols Advocat' residing in that cabinet – a concession by his mother one Christmas to the no alcohol rule, always stringently kept ever since his father's demise.

Attention was once again focused on Uncle Frank, Dicken's paternal uncle. 'Would you like some tea, Dicken?'

'Err... yes, thank you, I will.' Dicken was slightly disturbed, nervous, his eyelids heavy.

As Uncle Frank poured the tea into china cups, Dicken realised that this was not the same Number 10 he remembered; Uncle Frank was most definitely not the same Uncle Frank. This one was spotlessly clean, covered in cologne, and a touch too confident in his surroundings; certainly no dinner stains down the front of his shirt.

Dicken sat down. 'Cigarette, Dicken?' A box was proffered! A box!

'Yes, yes, thank you.' Dicken was shaken not only by the silver box, but by the fact that his uncle was smoking cork-tipped cigarettes – he had always smoked 'Golden Virginia' roll-ups. The image of his nicotine-stained fingers, picking... No, don't even go there.

'You don't look well, Dicken. You look old,' Uncle Frank said this as he handed Dicken his cup of tea, and added, 'Have you come far?' The menace in this statement, curled weed-like round the words.

Dicken found the whole situation ludicrous, it was only a dream after all. Dicken found himself answering, 'Well I am nearly thirty-two you know, Uncle.'

'Are you now? Isn't that strange. My, my – how very odd.' Uncle Frank did not look so friendly anymore. 'And where did you say you had come from, Dicken?' He looked puzzled now.

'Well... Uncle, you're not going to believe this, but I came from the year 1990. I live in Swaziland at the moment, and I think to be honest this is just a dream.' Dicken, at that very moment, wanted to wake up.

'A dream? How interesting, Dicken... More tea?'

Dicken's cup rattled on the saucer as he handed it to his uncle. When the cup returned, Dicken was stunned to notice two gold bands on his uncle's wedding finger – they had an ethereal quality about them, misty, almost floating above the skin in anticipation.

'So, you live in Swaziland, Dicken, and now you are a man. Are you married? Any children?' There was a look of intense interest on Uncle Frank's face, palpable salivation in fact, had he been a starving dog.

'No... I'm not married and there are no children.' Dicken tried to say this with as much energy as he could; he could feel his eyelids drooping further – the fatigue of his journey was beginning to catch up with him. Dicken knew something was wrong – this was only a dream and yet he knew he must stay awake, at all costs. This Uncle Frank was up to something – he couldn't be trusted.

'You look very tired... Would you like to go to your room?'

Dicken came to a start – he had nodded off. 'No! No!' He had detected an authority in his uncle's voice, a command. 'I can dictate this dream, Uncle Frank, not you. It's my dream, and you're dead!' Dicken was shouting and had leapt to his feet. This was now seriously frightening.

'Still the ill-mannered little brat, I see,' Uncle Frank was softly mocking.

Dicken sensed he had to get out, before... He was too late, Uncle Frank struck him full in the face with the teapot and Dicken tumbled off the chair he had been sitting on. As he struggled to get up Uncle Frank's boot came down heavily on his chest.

'You are not going anywhere, my lad; we have a few scores to settle – don't you remember?'

The earlier affability was gone; grim determination was set hard in the watery blue eyes. 'You see, Dicken, this is not exactly a dream, and I am afraid you do not dictate terms here; this is my house now, not your mother's, she's my wife.'

Dicken was convulsed with fear. 'No, that's not true, Mother would never have married you, never!'

'Ah... but she did, Dicken, after your death.'

'My death?! But I'm not dead. You're the one who is dead!' Dicken was still pinned to the floor.

'In a manner of speaking that's true, but only in your time. Perhaps you have forgotten you are in my time, and I'm very much alive, and my dream was always to marry your mother, even in death...'

Dicken's head was spinning, he felt sick. He must wake up.

Uncle Frank became more animated. 'You see, Dicken, if I kill you, the thirty-two year old you, your weakened spirit in a time you least belong, is mine to do with as I wish, and my wish will be for you to kill the thirteen-year-old brat who thwarted my desires – do you see?'

'But you are not real, this nightmare is only a dream...' Dicken was blubbing and could barely control his terror.

'Yes Dicken, you are right, but dreams sometimes are more than they seem, and spirits are eternal. Just as you could see the future of those whose homes you passed, so I can see yours. Your heart is weak, you are unhealthy, you could die in your sleep – then you are mine. But I need your spiritual presence alive for a few hours to do the deed.'

The clock struck the half hour – 3.30pm. 'Let us begin your nightmare, Dicken – let us see what ghosts can do. My prize as you see is too great for me to lose now – you have returned to haunt my eternal fantasy and in turn I have you – now I shall turn my fantasy into a reality. Your former triumph and my defeat will be reversed. I've hated you all these years, and in death I loathe you, arrogant, spoilt little nothing.'

Uncle Frank pounced on Dicken, his fingers tightened about the puffy throat – strong, military fingers. Dicken lashed out, but his blows were like paper aeroplanes in the wind. Through the window

Dicken could see the apple tree of his youth dancing, twisting, gyrating – his childhood flooding – night after night its limbs had tortured him on the wall, probing, gnarled fingers in the dark. The image was dimming, gasping for air.

'Frank! Frank! Stop it! Stop it at once!' In the doorway stood Dicken's mother.

Uncle Frank was on his feet. 'Get out woman, get out!' He was pushing her from the room.

Dicken clawed himself to the window; he had escaped Uncle Frank once before by this means. The catch was stiff, but the window gave way on the window ledge. The struggle at the door went on. Dicken was out – fresh air. Clean fresh air.

Uncle Frank bellowed. 'No! No! You can't escape!'

Dicken sprinted the length of the garden and over the back fence into the waste ground behind. Uncle Frank was after him. Dicken zigzagged through the tall, razor-sharp grass – it whipped his knees, tore at his clothes, exposed flesh!

Blood, trickling, dripping. Dripping. No. A big red ball, must get on, must get on. Uncle Frank snatching, snapping, frothing at the mouth. There, I'm up. Dicken safe. Must tread the ball, keep it going, getting tired. But I'm safe so long as I keep the ball turning. No blood must touch the ground. Keep the ball turning.

'Come down from there, Dicken, I was only joking.' A soft, warm, soothing Uncle Frank voice. 'Come down Dicken, it's all right now.' The calm words could not disguise the rage and loathing in his uncle's eyes.

Dicken wanted to live – he knew instinctively he had to stay there till 4.00pm – he had to – that's when Dicken junior arrived home from school. Dicken senior's heart was wincing, pumping – ten minutes to four.

Uncle Frank dancing, wild with rage, stabbing at the ball with a bread knife. Dicken remembering all those years before, May 1971.

'Will you marry me, Madge?' Oh how well Dicken remembered. Uncle Frank in sports jacket, dinner stained, too much tripe and cabbage. 'Will you?'

'Frank, Frank. I'll have to have to... ask the children.'

Alison, Corinne, Mark, and Dicken all standing there in silence – in fear.

Uncle Frank menacing.

Alison. 'Yes Mum, it's okay,' thinking of money for dances, although, she'd soon be gone.

Corrine. 'Yes Mum, it's okay,' thinking of all the clothes he'd promised her.

Mark. 'Yes Ma, it's okay,' thinking if it didn't work out he could leave home anyway – get the flat Frank had promised him.

'Dicken?' Mum asked, pleading. Uncle Frank menacing, drunk, violent, dirty, smelly Uncle Frank – why would he want him as a step-father?

Dicken. 'No... no I don't want you to, I don't want another dad. No, I hate him, no... no... no...'

'You little bastard, get off that ball, get off.' Just some blood, just a little – it will be enough.

The gate swung open; over the fence, Dicken saw the boy.

'Mum, Mum, I'm home.' Thin, mop headed and cheery – the whole of his life before him.

Dicken senior fell from the bloodied, red ball – he drifted into a deep and peaceful sleep. Uncle Frank could not touch him – dejected, beaten, he climbed the fence, and walked pitifully up the path, back to the house of 1971.

A bewildered Madge stared in recognition at the prostrate, bleeding figure on the other side of the fence as it faded from view, then quickly she spun about face and marched into the house.

Dicken hovered the house for a while in a stupor, then he was on a 391 bus to town; all the neighbours were aboard, all smiling faintly, vaguely disappointed, knowing. Then Dicken woke up.

'Thank God I was not late home,' murmured Dicken, and got up for a glass of water. As he entered the living room the clock struck its fourth chime. By the front door, obviously pushed under from the outside, was an envelope. Dicken looked at the envelope on the floor for a moment then went to pick it up.

The aroma of 'Golden Virginia' tobacco assailed his nostrils, and his body began to quiver – the spidery handwriting was distinctive, the contents, a simple message. 'You bastard, Next time...!'

Dicken placed the envelope and the note on the table. It was then he caught sight of the post date, May 22 1971 – the calendar on the wall told him it was May 21st 1990.

Dicken vowed that morning before dawn never to eat the previous night's combination again – Marmite and cheese were clearly safe, salad cream and cheese were not – and then he remembered Uncle Frank's aversion to salad cream and lest he make the same mistake again, which he conceivably might, he made himself a second promise. In future a sensible diet, and a course in martial arts!

3

Forgotten

A cold, crisp morning in late autumn. I met her that morning for the first time... a large, bulbous lady... Surrounded by her memories and the wreckage of too many ready meals for one. There was more of course, a vague odour of corruption... the domestic kind; too little movement... comfortable but worn chair to grimy sink and on to greasy cooker... inhabited by a solitary, battered kettle constantly on the boil. Copious glasses of purified, scalding water to ease the terrible indigestion of comfort eating in the dead of night. No breakfast in evidence but an overflowing, pungent ashtray, conformation perhaps of the sleepless night that had gone before. The greyness of her skin and the hollow look in her eyes masked almost successfully by the bright, cheery hello and the smile... such a wonderful smile that revealed a life before this rather disturbing existence. She had fallen so far and yet it had been gradual, so much so that neither she nor her occasional visitors took much notice anymore. The newcomer was welcomed into this world of medication and steam and invited to sit down.

So many years of loneliness, piled high with the embellished lives of the rich and famous, TAKE A BREAK... She had not rushed headlong into their world, found comfort in their excess, only surfacing to imbibe on her hot water and salivate over Captain Birdseye's chemical concoctions. About her lay the ruin of her past life, covered in dust and neglect. Brown photographs in battered frames... badly dressed ancestors wreathed in uncomfortable smiles, a dinner service, almost hidden behind filthy glass. Bills and letters from anonymous utilities carpeting a concrete floor. A kitchen table, the mantle for her drug-assisted state... all manner of pills, potions and lotions to supplicate, to deflect her real needs... love and tenderness, conversation, animation. She had been slumped in that grotesque and stinking chair when I arrived that morning. We spoke briefly about her needs for the garden and I then set about my task. As I headed for the tumble down shed she moved to the window, leaning heavily on the sill. I glanced back and waved... a tentative gesture, reciprocated with that nervous, girlish smile.

The next hour passed quickly and the unkempt lawns were transformed... a kind of order restored amid the borders, rank with weeds. I stopped for a moment and wiped away the sweat that had trickled down into the corners of my eyes and then looked up. She was out on the scrubby path, regarding me with some concern.

'Stop for a while, John... take a break...' she called out, and then she turned and shuffled back inside. I switched off the ancient mower and made my way back up to the house. As I entered the kitchen I noted the change in the quality of the air... green apples and honeysuckle... air freshener... and the room was empty, her stale smell expunged, banished by CFCs.

'MISS LAST...? MISS LAST, are you there?' She appeared at the door that led out into the hallway. She had changed her clothes. The grubby sweatshirt had been replaced by a bright pink, furry jumper and her food-stained sweatpants by a pair of black slacks. Her hair, steely grey and unwashed had been slicked back and tidied with a comb. She looked more confident and at ease. She moved stiffly into the room and settled herself into that horrible chair. It groaned as she shifted her bulk and reached for her cigarette tin. She lit the paper at the end and it fizzed briefly, then glowed as she sucked heavily; the ash crept steadily up the stem and she puffed out a stream of acrid vapour. She spoke... a deep, husky, rasping voice.

'You'll do, I think... Tell me about yourself, have

you always been a gardener?' The rest of the visit passed in conversation and me finishing the lawns at the front of the house. Three hours had gone by and at least half of that time had been spent chatting, mainly about me and a bit of comment on current news. She paid me for my time and watched me drive away, the mask stripped away and the sadness back in place.

'Call me Maggie,' she said on my second visit, and so I did. I knew Maggie only a short while, perhaps eighteen months, but in that time she touched a chord in my life and her memories, thoughts, and observations are etched into my own. Ostensibly I was her gardener – three hours a fortnight – but as time went on I found myself, almost unconsciously, spending a further two hours at least, chatting – knowing I should be on my way to another job but finding myself just sitting there and continuing to swap stories. She was always waiting for me, always cheerful, despite being clearly in pain. Her beauty lay in her smile and her dirty laugh. She told me stories of her life, illuminating the faded trinkets and images of that kitchen room, its squalor swept away by the remembrance of her childhood, her lost loves and the events that shaped her existence. I began to understand her withdrawal, the closed doors and the sadness when I left. For a few hours she had a confidant, someone to listen and to listen to. We discussed events in the news – football and the Iraq war – she wasn't very impressed with Tony Blair or George Bush. She felt very deeply about the loss of rural life, the nature cycle of the seasons, the festivals she had felt had been debased – all blurred by the mad rush that we now live in. She could not fathom how careless the world had become. And all the time the hot water would be sipped; never once did I ask what all the medication was for. We just settled into a gentle routine, a spell of gardening, chat, then more gardening and then more chat. Over time our stories deepened and the detail was no longer shallow. We trusted one another, we had become friends.

She grew up in a small village in the Home Counties and lived her whole life there – I don't believe she ever travelled far over the years – a trip to Scotland once by coach with a friend and visits to relatives in Devon in her younger days, and yet she was knowledgeable, wise and without prejudice; she did not like extreme views and had no patience with people who thought themselves better than others. Her farming days were, I think, the happiest – so many stories. Funny, sad, occasionally wild, but always tempered with a message – a simple one – a message to us all: life is short, whether we die young or old, time passes us by and we forget or put off the words and stories our hearts want to tell. Maggie never expressed regrets, she accepted how her life had panned out and just got on with it. Her body had grown old and she creaked a bit but her mind was alive, there was urgency about her words and each time I left, a frustration that she had no time to tell me more.

I did not see she was going to die, I suppose I should have known had I considered the vast array of medication that floated about the kitchen table and the fact that her beloved motorbike sat quietly festering in the yard, but I didn't and consciously neither did she. Christmas was approaching and she was ready: all her cards were written and family birthdays clearly marked for the month of December; plans for the holiday period and beyond were in place. The video had finally been fixed, logs were stacked in the shed, insurance and tax paid on the motorbike, just in case... She had been so happy a few weeks previous when she had sorted out a rebate on her council tax. She had handed in an old shotgun in the summer, worried about the safety of it, and had survived a pair of bogus callers. She was a tough old bird and had not long started receiving her official pension. The summer before her death we had cut logs together, her wielding the chainsaw like a true professional. How could I have imagined she would die? And yet in her last days the urgency of her conversation had abated; we sometimes just sat in comfortable silence after I had finished my stint in the garden.

A phone call one evening gave me the news of Maggie's death, a massive heart attack a few days previously. She had been found by her niece and on the following Saturday morning I returned the keys Maggie had given me back in the summer, just in case I couldn't rouse her... The funeral was held at a local crematorium on the Monday. I arrived early and round the back of the building lay the vast expanse of the town cemetery, where a couple of years before I had attended the funeral of an old childhood friend. I chose to visit him and remember. Fine rain was falling by now and I made my way back to the chapel and the funeral party filed in. Maggie was carried in and laid before us in her simple coffin, adorned with a single wreath. The family mainly sat down one side. So many faces I did not know but the names and the stories crowded in on me; stories told with love and concern. Maggie cared deeply about her family – uncles, aunts, nieces and nephews and cousins. She would search out photographs of decades ago – pictures of her grandparents, her mum and dad, her brothers, all long gone and yet still vibrant in her memory. She would tell me their stories, their joys and sorrows, their winters and summers. She reminded me of cherished childhood games, long forgotten. Her mind was sharp and her words stung with poignancy as she described the characters she had met and the life of the village as it once had been. She explained, in detail, how farming changed so rapidly over a period of a few short years and how it destroyed the community she had grown up with. She spoke of evenings in the pub and visits to markets and fairs, of family mealtimes and the bartering of skills and food.

She minded a little that those times had passed, but more wondered where we were going and why we had lost our ability to really listen to one another; she wondered where all the time had gone and then smiled and said she knew. The last years of her life were lonely but there was no bitterness, and yet I felt angry when she died because progress was taken from us, with increasing ferocity, the time we need to listen and learn. I was fortunate to chance upon Maggie and was fascinated by her simple but full life. I am glad that I met her and knew her for those two summers. I shall miss her and the 'Morning John!' followed by that deep, throaty chuckle. I hope there is a heaven and at this moment she is zooming about on her scooter in the sky, free from the pain she endured, looking down on us all with her radiant smile. Goodbye Maggie, and thank you for making my life richer in understanding.

4

Miss Arabella's Short Retirement...

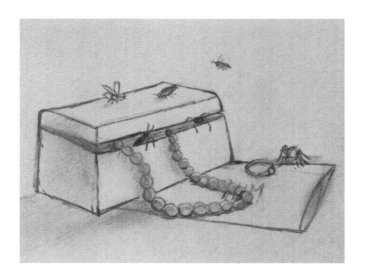

Miss Arabella Stuart stepped gingerly off the plane, her whole retirement spread out before her. She was healthy and sprightly for her age and was determined to make a fresh start... Fleetingly she thought about what she had left behind and whether her decision had been the right one, and then the image of dreary, cold and wet Dagenham dispelled her doubts. The sun was blazing down and the faces she met were friendly and cheery. Marching smartly into Arrivals and up to the official on the door she gave a little skip... carefree and contented, that's what she would be, despite a nagging feeling – only slight – that she was walking into danger...

She could see her nephew, Georgie. She waved happily... then something bit her.

'Ouch!' she yelped. Some nasty little insect had seen her soft, pudgy flesh coming and had settled for his early lunch. She passed through Customs without too much bother, collected her single case and greeted Georgie with a warm smile, showing perhaps a little of the relief that the long journey was over.

The car was just outside and they were soon on their way... 'Did you get bitten?' Georgie asked, noting Arabella was furiously scratching her arm...

'Yes,' muttered Arabella, 'but don't fuss, Georgie dear, mosquitoes are bothersome creatures but I will get used them. I assume that's what it was.'

They were soon at the family home and were met at the gates by Ben... the watchie... What exactly he was guarding in such an isolated spot puzzled Arabella. The garden was a wilderness and the house looked ramshackle and rather uncared for... sinister even. Lucy, Georgie's wife, emerged from the house as the car pulled up. That silly, rather irritating, twitchy face was still the same... a face that needed to be smacked, Arabella momentarily thought, and then was deliciously shocked by such wickedness.

'Hello darling Aunt Arabella... did you have a good trip? You look a little tired.'

Arabella was tired and her arm was sore, and beginning to swell. Lucy didn't wait for an answer. Instead she bustled her into the rambling house... inside was more chaotic even than the overgrown gardens... and no less disturbing.

Mavis, the maid, snatched up her suitcase and shuffled off into the depths of the house. Lucy ushered Arabella across the room and settled her on a grubby and slightly damp sofa. 'Nice cup of tea on the way, Auntie.'

A few moments later she tottered in with a dull-looking silver tray. The battered teapot and chipped cups looked decidedly uninviting and the brown sludge that ended up in the cups was quite revolting, but Arabella was thirsty... She drank greedily... and almost at once regretted it.

I think Arabella may have made the biggest mistake of her life... I may be wrong, mind...

At that moment, Jimmy and Pamela came bursting into the room; they stopped dead in their tracks when they saw Arabella... 'Say hello to Auntie,' chimed Lucy and Georgie together. The two children glanced warily at the sickly looking 'chubster' on the sofa and then smiled sweetly and said, 'Helloow.' That was all, and then they were gone. Into an adjoining room... as the door closed Arabella imagined, surely, a glittering, gleeful cruelty in their eyes. Behind the closed door she could hear muffled giggling and rummaging... and then they were back... emerging into the gloomy room, both carrying a little black lacquered box each. They stood silently for a few seconds then looked towards their parents. 'Can we show Aunt Bella our collections?'

Lucy Moyse smiled faintly and nodded to her husband. 'Very well darlings, but only a quick peek. Auntie is tired and should really be in bed after such a long journey.'

The two children ceremoniously laid their boxes on the rickety tea table in front of Arabella. 'I will go first,' said Jimmy, pushing Lucy roughly to the floor... As she fell, he snatched open his box. Arabella was horrified because there, neatly displayed, were a variety of dead spiders and beetles, all neatly pinned to a dusty velvet lining. Suddenly she saw the gleam of malice in his smirking pride. He then snapped the box shut and nudged the now standing Lucy. Too shocked to say anything, Arabella waited for Pamela's surprise package. Quite delicately, the little girl proudly lifted her lid... inside were all manner of squashed and shattered butterflies and moths. Congealed in rancid face cream... Arabella's disgust was complete. What ghastly brats they were, and as they turned to go she detected for the first time the sour odour of the unwashed. Her nostrils wrinkled...

'Don't mind them, Auntie... they just like collecting little things they find round the house. It amuses them,' smiled Georgie with a faint sneer on his face...

'Couldn't they collect something a little less gruesome?' Arabella muttered.

You just know Arabella is going to regret her decision...

'They could, Auntie dearest... but they're not going to,' Georgie barked in retort and fixed her with an intent and ugly stare. Throughout all of this Lucy had remained fearfully silent... but suddenly sprung into life.

'Well Auntie... you must be awfully tired. Time for you to see where you are to sleep. I will show you to your room so you can freshen up for dinner. About half an hour, shall we say...?'

Lucy led Arabella along various unlit and increasingly dusty and smelly passages, and finally stopped at a door bearing the name Great Aunt Bella, scrawled in black felt tip pen on a grubby and torn piece of old newspaper. 'The children thought it would make you feel welcome... wasn't that a nice gesture?' Bella, as seemingly that was her name, thought it creepy and was rather daunted by what she was about to find in this room, but dutifully answered, 'Indeed... a lovely gesture.'

Lucy swung the door open and propelled Bella inside. What met her eyes was extraordinary in the extreme, in that it was so opposite to the rest of the house that she had seen. The chamber was elegantly decorated and tastefully furnished. Flowers adorned the dresser and the bedside table, and the fragrance gave the room a dreamy quality...

'I hope you like it, Auntie,' said Lucy, somewhat nervously, glancing quickly in all the corners per chance the children had not left any unwelcome presents.

'Oh, it is glorious Lucy... what a heavenly room... thank you so much.'

Lucy relaxed a little and then turned heel and parted with the words, 'Dinner in twenty minutes, Jimmy will come and collect you.' And with that the door was firmly closed and... locked!! Arabella was startled, but so very tired, and just plumped down on the bed and sighed... 'Well, well, they have done me proud.' And yet the door locked and she had the feeling that all was not well in this strange house. Georgie had changed so much since she had last seen him and Lucy was like a frightened rabbit... and the two children were decidedly odd, nay, slightly malevolent...

Arabella was uncomfortable already in their company. They had all unnerved her... each in their way... and there was a definite fear growing in her that things were only going to get worse for her... Why the locked door?

She rose from the bed and walked to the barred window. The garden, though overgrown and now in half-light, was still quite pretty and for a moment held her attention... Her trance was rudely broken by a pair of wild, grinning yellow teeth at the window, broken and encrusted in the grime of half-eaten food... Bella stepped back in utter panic...

'Hello Miss Bella... I am Thomas... the gardener, just so you know.' He wanted her to open the window... tapping on the glass and leering in... He was frightening her and yet she did as he bid. Almost immediately his hand was in and grabbing hers, grasping and stroking hers vigorously... too tight and too roughly... Finally he let go and instantly disappeared from view. She shut the window smartly as she heard him rush away, gibbering to himself. Or was he actually cackling as he crashed through the tangled shrubbery?

Arabella pulled herself away from the window and went to wash her face and hands... She was sweating profusely... As an afterthought she applied some lipstick and a dab of scent, and then brushed her hair. She then unpacked and changed for dinner. The fatigue was growing and she settled herself in a deep chair as far away from the window as possible and drifted off into deep thought... Her mind was made up... she couldn't stay here... It was awful. She would start looking for a property the very next day. She had more than enough money... she may even start writing her memoirs... but first she knew she had to get away... she was in danger, she knew it.

Her eyes felt heavy and just as they began to droop the door was unlocked and Jimmy slammed the door wide and appeared and stood hands on hips... 'Mummy says dinner is served and I'm to take you, Auntie Bells... now... Oh and I'm to say sorry about my frightening you with my spidery box, though actually I'm not really, Bellykins...' And with that he pinched her cheek rather roughly and smiled affectionately, and then muttered something that sounded like, 'Come on you old cash cow.' But he couldn't have said that, could he? She must have misheard...

'Jimmy I wasn't frightened by your box... just a little surprised.'

The boy frowned and looked disappointed... even angry... and there it was again. 'Old bitch... You'll be sorry you ever came.' No, he really couldn't have said that! Then without further ado he snatched up her hand and dragged her into the dark and dusty passage. The musty smell was much stronger now and as her other hand touched the peeling wallpaper – it was dripping wet and seemed to come away with crumbling plaster, alive with all sorts of crawling insects... He was pulling her along at a ferocious speed and she was barely able to keep up... He reached the dining room and pushed her in...

'The old slut is here then,' said a menacing voice from a dim corner of the room... It was Georgie, surely. 'Drink, Auntie Bell... and some lovely dinner and a rather important little chat I think.'

The crickets had begun to chatter outside and the room was bathed in candlelight. Pungent odours rose softly from the table top and Bella's spine tingled...

Tentatively Bella sat down, and despite the strange smells that wafted up from the table the food was actually very good, but the candles were stinging her eyes, and through the haze her concerns were growing. The idle chatter was all about the weather and the state of the economy in Britain and the rise of new political parties like UKIP, and how she viewed such matters... It was all tedious and Bella knew it was leading up to conversation... no pronouncements. Dinner was over... no dessert... and Georgie indicated they retire to the living room for coffee and brandy. Over the brandy Georgie cleared his throat and began the expected lecture... *More like orders*, Bella thought...

'Now Auntie, just a few things before we retire for bed. I had best say from the outset that you will find things rather strange at first and I suggest most strongly that you do not venture out in the dark alone... ever. If you want to go into town Lucy or myself will take you... You mustn't walk out alone around here, even in daylight.' Before Bella had time to respond, he continued, 'As a precaution I lock all doors, even the uninhabited ones... at all times, so don't be alarmed if your door is locked tonight. It is our way and keeps us all safe.'

So I am to be a prisoner. But why? Bella was confused and alarmed, but there was no way she could respond. She felt terribly sick and so very tired.

'Oh yes, and one final thing... The rest will keep... we rise for breakfast at seven. Jimmy will collect you. Now I will be away to my bed. Lucy, come now... night Auntie, sleep soundly.' And with that parting the odd couple disappeared into the gloom. Arabella was stunned. She was almost certain they were all slightly deranged. She had wanted to ask so many questions but no chance had been given, he had been so officious and rude. The room was now empty and she slumped back in the chair and rested her weary body. Another brandy to fortify herself... *A stiff one*, she thought.

Almost immediately though, just as the amber liquid fell gently into the glass, Mavis, the stumpy maid, appeared and promptly blew out the candles... 'You are to go to bed now, please. I will show you the way... Come now.' So the brandy was left untouched and she felt a rough tug at her arm, strong and insistent. Unable to resist, Arabella rose and followed obediently... She did not relish getting lost in the myriad of passages, full of their unsavoury surprises.

A thought struck Arabella... *No children at the meal...* 'Mavis, may I ask... where do the children normally eat?'

Mavis scowled. 'They eat in the kitchen, Miss Bella... and you will kindly ask no further questions. The business of the family is not yours to know.' The rank odour of the passage to her room was stronger, foul in fact. They quickly reached the door to her room, now minus the scrawled note. Mavis swung the door open and pushed Arabella forcibly inside and slammed the door firmly shut... A whispered conversation ensued... the key turned and the muffled words continued briefly, then footsteps padded of in different directions. So that was it... prisoner till morning. The room was silent. Even the garden noises had ceased. Arabella shivered and lit the solitary candle provided, undressed and clambered into bed. She really was too tired to think too much about the strangeness she had encountered thus far. She was soon deeply asleep... dreams full of ugly, crushed insects.

The sputtering candle woke her... and the sweltering heat of the room... The air was heavy with the perfume of the flowers and their odour was overpowering, catching at the back of her throat... oppressive... choking in the heat... Oh my... Oh no... the windows were open, and with a rush of wind they were in. All kinds of buzzing and flapping of wings. Her room was a battleground and she was the target. Whatever they were, she was the prey... She heard the distant cackling of various, faint voices and then felt the swarm envelop her... biting... crawling... slipping down her throat... She screamed until she could scream no more. She collapsed... her heart had given out... result!

The door opened and the whole family entered; Jimmy and Pamela armed with boxes of pins... rather large pins. Lucy closed the windows and Georgie rifled through Arabella's bag...

'Dear Aunt Bella... always so generous... so

wonderfully generous!'

Two days later Arabella was found in a ditch on the outskirts of the town, near a sheebeen, her throat cut and her personal belongings strewn over quite a large area... The police concluded she had been mugged and murdered when she put up a fight. Georgie had reported her missing the night after she died... he had, apparently, been in a terrible state. He had told her not to go out alone... why hadn't she listened? He had complained bitterly.

Sometime later Georgie travelled to England for the reading of the will. It had been changed two weeks before Arabella's departure from England and foolishly she had informed him by letter... The letter had arrived the week before... a whole week for the destitute family to prepare...

5

Vusie

Endless nights Vusie sat up guarding a car – a car that was not his. Why, he could not tell, but he did – he thought his father irresponsible when he chuckled, 'Safe as houses, Vusie.'

It was worse on nights when it rained; every sound, the fall of a twig, a car passing in the night, the irregular chant of the crickets and toads – all made him alert. His heart would start to pound, his fingers tingle, numbness would engulf his body. Fear and anger would then become one; his muscles would throb, his mouth would set hard, and then to the window he would go, and peer furtively out. The family would stir in their beds and he would start, and pull sharply back.

This was Swaziland in the year 1990. Vusie's father had contracted a firm to erect a six foot fence around their modest property – it would run down the length of the mango trees, and along the front of the garden; the banana trees would have to go. The fence would cost his father the best part of two months' salary, and that was only because he knew the fellow who ran the firm – a favour, his father had called it! A gate would also be installed, one with a large and very solid padlock.

Vusie thought back a few short years – then there was peace at night. You know only the toads and crickets were abound – their noise regular and confident. Now it was not so, even they were nervous, unsure.

A sinister, and dangerously new element had crept into town life, almost unnoticed, certainly unchecked. It had exploded into a frenzied orgy of vicious violation; theft on a scale previously unimagined. Theft accompanied by a barbarism unknown to the Swazi – violence, cruelty, even murder if need be. The police seemed powerless to stop the wholesale theft of cars; some said that the upholders of the law were intimately involved themselves; though Vusie knew this to be an exaggeration, he also believed that a minority of the men in blue did indeed have their itchy fingers deep in this murky, but lucrative pie. The general public professed a knowledge of the perpetrators of these crimes, teachers knew the names of their students lured into this ugly trade by greed, and the undeniable glamour it beheld – and yet all were silent. Why? Unbelievable fear – fear of the guns, of the knives, of the brutal beatings.

Vusie was scared for his family – it had begun with the proliferation of vicious burglaries in 1989 – the death of countless innocent people, old and young. Axe murders for a badly made radio and a few blankets; stabbings and shootings for a clapped-out old car, which would shudder to a halt some months later on a war-torn road in Mozambique. Many had died in the defence of their property, others maimed in brutal attacks after the sidlanis had taken what they had come for – afterthoughts which included the rape of old and young alike.

Vusie had read a poem once about 'gentlemen in the night' – it had frightened him terribly, but now he fully understood what 'gentlemen in the night' could do. And the 'gentlemen' of Swaziland were certainly not gentlemen. Dawn was always a long time in coming when Vusie was on watch.

Vusie's father had worked for ten long years for that car – hard years that denied the buying of Christmas presents for the children, or even a new dress for his wife. It was the only real material possession the family had to show for all that time. As Vusie looked around the room he noted the drab, mismatched armchairs – threadbare, torn beyond repair in some places; they really were most uncomfortable chairs, the springs had long since ceased to do what they should. He saw the floor, cold, bare and grey, smooth from the daily scrubbing it received from his mother's gnarled and rough hands. The house had been left to them by his grandfather, a kind and tender old man; it wasn't big, nor was it particularly well-built – rooms had been added as the family grew in size. Vusie thought of his mother, those sad and loving eyes, her sagging breasts, her small body worn out from the cooking, scrubbing, suckling and weeding – her back overly curved for a woman of her age. Saturday was her day now that they had a car – off to Nhlangano or Hlatikulu to visit her widowed mother, or relatives – a day of joy, and never a cross word. Days of warmth and renewal, leaving a glow that shimmered for the whole week after; if the car were to be stolen there would be no more trips, the bus was too expensive. Vusie screwed up his eyes tightly as he thought what such a thing would do to his mother – she would pine, and finally die. The drudgery of life would strike her down, break her soul, give her to a god that Vusie neither trusted nor understood. Insurance was high in Swaziland and Vusie's father was not covered for theft; Vusie only knew that the car must be protected at all costs.

As the hands of the clock danced jerkily forward Vusie remembered his father telling him of old times gone by when cars could be left open by hurrying shoppers, of money left on seats, of honesty unbounded. No one dreamt of stealing what did not belong to them. More likely an upstanding Swazi citizen would find the owner and tell them of their forgetfulness. Theft in those days was caused by physical hunger, his father had said, and Vusie smiled to himself when remembering his father's story of the man who was so hungry he broke into the house of a local magistrate and cooked himself a meal, taking care not to make a mess, and even washing up afterwards!

Vusie mused on the progress of today, the European and American influence through film, radio, and television and the change in values that accompanied the progress and influence, creeping like a cancerous stranger. Progress seemed evil to Vusie, he knew it wasn't, but it had created with all its goodness, a darkness, a side of nature now and threatening; it had unsettled and corrupted his people.

Now people locked their doors, chained up their cars, fitted burglar bars and alarms, employed watchmen with batons and lived in fear of the darkness. Where Vusie lived there were no watchmen – there were houses all around his own, but no door opened when the sun went to bed, heavy bolts slammed noisily across doors, and when a fellow human being was in trouble curtains would twitch and friends would shrink away, go to their beds, pull the covers tightly up around their necks and shiver at the ghostly thoughts that sped to the pit of their conscience – hoping, praying, begging that the intruders would not come for them too. Vusie knew he had to take a stand.

Was this the Swaziland of his early childhood? It certainly was not, but it was reality, the here and now, and Vusie felt desperately alone. Until the fence was up he could not sleep; to his credit though his limbs would ache and his body sweat hot and cold, he never allowed his eyelids to droop. The shadows outside, the murmuring trees, the cough of his little brother, the dogs stirring and barking at falsehoods, all kept him very much wide awake, on guard with a knobkerrie he never wished to use. His grandfather and his father had taught him that violence was cowardly, evil, against God; it was ugly and stupid, and yet what was he to do if a 'gentleman of the night' passed by? Or two, or three!

Each night Vusie lingered, wishing the fence was there, even praying that the all-seeing untrustworthy God would magic it there. Some nights when the lids on Vusie's eyes felt uncommonly heavy he would imagine he could see it there. Before they had the car Vusie loved nothing better than to hear the breeze rushing into his bedroom through the unfilled cracks in the putty. Now he hated the rain, and at times, when it hammered on the leaky roof and went *drip, drip,* he would whisper to himself, 'God, take this abomination away.' He knew he didn't mean it, he learnt abomination was a word associated with the devil, and the rain was God's life-giver, so how could it be? But, in Vusie's circumstances it did mean only one thing – thieves, sidlanis abroad, skulking in the oily, moonless night, under cover of the *drip, drip, drip.* On nights such as these he would draw his chair closer to the window, but make sure the catch was fastened, so no stealthy hand could enter and grab him; he would visualise a peaceful, undisturbed sleep, but shake himself and pinch his face or bite his tongue.

Vusie was fourteen years old, and slightly built; he didn't go hungry, in fact his mother berated him for eating too much – his sinewy frame exuded youth and hope. He was reserved, polite, and respected his elders, though once he nearly lost that respect when a drunken old man punched his mother to the ground while she was still heavy with Sipho, his younger brother. The drunk had shouted at Vusie's mother, leered and spat at her, and called her unmentionable names when she had cried in indignation. He had wagged his finger at her and muttered something about showing respect for elders. He had cuffed Vusie around the ear and had launched a kick in the direction of the prostrate mother's belly. Vusie, incensed, had been restrained by a Member of Parliament, an elderly man himself, who had been walking by and witnessed the whole dreadful incident. He had exploded into action, and had grabbed the sop's collar, kicking him hard on the shin as he did so. He had then propelled the fellow, flailing, into a newspaper seller, who had promptly slapped the crumpled heap hard across the face. Vusie had helped his shaken mother to her feet, resisting the urge to join the crowd that had gathered round the drunk to remonstrate with him. Vusie had felt violence was called for in that instance. He had wondered then what was happening to Manzini, once the hub of honest activity.

Vusie attended Salesian High School in Manzini, the mission school, and yet even there he saw the changes that were being noted in schools up and down the country; all the desks had padlocks and the boys were watchful of their possessions. Vile language punctuated lunch-times, mostly out of earshot of an ever-vigilant staff, but not always. Some boys dropped out of school because their minds were full of dagga and television pictures that told of wonderful riches to be had in America – violence and crime shown as an acceptable form of entertainment, a way of life. Films at Julie's cinema showing gratuitous death and sex as the norm – all lapped up by impressionable minds after school, when homework waited eagerly, but unlikely to be done.

Vusie read the newspapers that reported the madness in society; strikes, drunken drivers, horrendous road accidents, teachers taking advantage of silly young schoolgirls, cruelty to humans and animals alike, rape, theft of property and life – all shown as acceptable, or at least normal. Was it surprising then that his fellow students were changing? Fast cars, easy sex, no responsibilities, alcohol, flashing alluringly across the screens for all to salivate over. It was horrible, and Vusie was thankful that his family could not afford this 'youth-destroyer', this devil of progress, constantly preferring the good life. The newspapers only reflected the effect.

Vusie wasn't sure his mother was wholly right when she said, 'The magical-box is an agent of the devil.' He felt it didn't need to be, but he shuddered when he thought of his friend Themba, who had sat for hours on end watching South African TV with all its advertisements, and had at the end of form III, in utter depression, at only achieving a third class pass, hanged himself in the woods behind his parents' home. In his suicide note he had cried out that he was a failure, the TV had shown him how useless he was, how bad life was for those who weren't first. *Temba was a fool*, thought Vusie. TV was a dangerous fantasy, unreal, depicting lies. Themba, he remembered, had a great talent – he could sing, make anything with his hands, and could run like an express train. Vusie missed his friend – dagga and television had killed him.

Sipho needed schooling, and Vusie's sisters had only gone up to standard V. When Vusie qualified as a vet, for that was what he wanted to be, he would see to it that they all received what was due to them, what was due to every human being – education. His parents would be provided for – everything they ever wanted. He mused on their simple pleasures and wishes for the future. He would decorate their house and buy them comfortable furniture, and buy his mother a beautiful dress for her Saturday outings...

What was that! Vusie's hearing was acute; his daydreaming and deep thought evaporated abruptly. He heard the crunching of the gravel under sly, heavy footsteps – someone was approaching. His stick, where was it? On the other side of the room. Oh quick, quick... Vusie was at the window, the door keys were clenched tightly in his sweating palm. The other hand was welded to the stick, his father's knobkerrie. The candle had burnt out an hour or so earlier; the room was bathed in a silence, this pitch. They had come. *The car, oh my god, the car.* Vusie had dreaded this moment – week upon week he had waited, until his father could stand it no longer, and had said he would get the fence and the gate. Vusie's school report had been disturbing.

'He falls asleep; he is not attentive; he is late for school.'

Ever since the car had arrived Vusie had changed – nervous, jerky, sullen, were words to describe a once happy, well-adjusted boy.

Vusie watched, mesmerised, as the wiry spectre advanced on the car – the intruder bent down, and tested the chain – it was a good strong chain, wrapped round the axle, secured in concrete. 'Safe as houses,' his dad had said. It had to hold, it had to...

Piercing the deathly night came the sound of a

voice, husky, wheezing, commanding. 'Sizweee, the bolt cutters, be quick.'

Oh no! Please God. A scream, hysterical and full of terror, began to speed up Vusie's throat. 'Please God. No, no.'

The chain pinged.

The scream strangled in Vusie's throat – he had to act – the sidlanis were taking his father's precious car. A blister blotted out the fear in Vusie's brain. He was at the door; safety, life, forgotten. He struggled with the keys, they jangled like the dinner bell, grated in the lock; he flung the door to. His hot breath poured into the night sky, escaping into the nothingness. The thieves heard him and saw him coming. Screaming and charging, Vusie resembled a Zulu warrior in the days of Shaka.

The thugs stood their ground; the security light caught the glint of steel, drawn expertly and assuredly Vusie skidded to a halt on the slippery grass.

'Dog, little dog – have you no respect for your elders?'

Vusie's family were at the window – his father, panic-stricken, stood motionless, eyes wide; his mother's face encompassed the fear of the Swazi nation. The sidlanis had come, as she knew they always would.

'Get him Sizwe, slice the little runt.'

Sizwe advanced on Vusie; the one with the husky voice skirted around the car to the passenger side. Vusie jumped back as Sizwe lunged forward. The stick, for so long inactive, sprung into life. It swished through the air; there was a yelp of pain, and a clatter of steel against stone.

Vusie was upon him, clawing, biting, tearing, punching. The face became clear. Sizwe Vilakati! A thug from school, a dirty, greasy boy. A liar, a cheat, a bully... and now a thief. Energy surged into Vusie's taut limbs, blood pumped ferociously into his temples, all the silent, curdling hatred rose, massing, boiling until it erupted. The misery was released, and Sizwe lay senseless, moaning, begging, whining like a grizzling bloodied babe.

Still Vusie did not let go, squeezing, throat constricting...

'Mandlaaa.'

The car door was open; it slammed shut. Vusie let go! Sizwe rolled onto his stomach, gasping for air, then vomited, and was silent. The car roared into life, spluttered and died. Again and again it did this, and Vusie just stared. The engine cut out; the 'snake's' head disappeared beneath the dashboard.

Slowly the fury gathered pace, the fire burned, the heaving stopped – Vusie moved determinedly towards the car. His eardrums sang as the waves of seething bitterness rushed into the upraised knobkerrie; it fell like a giant boulder, crashing, a splintering crack – the figure in the car hopelessly trapped. Again the knobkerrie was raised, followed by a blood-curdling roar. The windscreen shattered, a dull thud; moaning softly, the purveyor of human indecency slumped heavily over the wheel. The side window fell to the might of Vusie's next blow – the stick was discarded – his urgent hand shot through the broken mess. Victory was near...

Pain, searing pain. Vusie felt the scalding torrent of blood, gushing from his wrist – a trick, a deception, what a fool! The intruder, Mandla, a boy who Vusie had once shared his lunch with, rose like a rampant mamba; spitting, foaming, slashing, laughing.

The door burst open and Vusie fell to the ground – no deception. Mandla was running, jumping like some mad dervish. Sizwe was staggering, whimpering, tottering to freedom. Vusie's war was over; he joined the night.

The stone statues in the living room came to life. Vusie's father ran wildly into the garden. His son was lifeless in his arms. He cradled his baby and stroked his soft hair.

'Oh Vusie. Why? Why? Safe as houses. I told you, son. Why? Why?'

Vusie died that night and with him a part of Swaziland perished. God stood by and watched, sadly receiving this young soul, so out of step with modern-day Swaziland. There are thousands of other good boys like Vusie – decent, honest, and full of hope – and quite a number of misguided fools like Themba, Sizwe, and Mandla, but we soon forget. Next time, maybe, you will be the victim, yes you behind the twitching curtains, or you in the government office, or yes even you Mr Policeman, or perhaps even you Mr Car Thief Baron, whoever you are. Or you, the paperclip thief, or you, the government car abuser.

Mandla died some months later trying to steal a video recorder – shot at point blank range. Sizwe and his boss, still lurk in the shadows...

Vusie is dead, but he was a true Swazi – think of your children, Swaziland, and what their future may be.

6

The Alternative Nativity

'Get 'er Rosie; get the little bitch...'

Rosie did as she was told... Ethel was bigger than her and a good deal stronger. The two girls, sisters, had nabbed Daphne Boot, the road sweeper's daughter. Daphne was good at school... Ethel and

Rosie were not... and hated Daphne with a passion.

'Bloody little liar, dirty little cow.' Daphne was terrified, Ethel was angry. Rosie always did as she was told.

'Get me into trouble would yer? You little slut. I saw yer... didn't I Rosie?'

Rosie nodded and flicked her long, dirty, greasy hair from her from her eyes... wide and frightened. Ethel's eyes were narrow and cruel... *Piggy eyes*, thought Daphne, as she was thrown roughly to the ground. She could smell the freshly cut grass for just a moment and then Ethel landed on her... heavily. The sweet smell of grass faded quickly, replaced by the rancid odour of Ethel's lardy sweat... mingling with the fishy perfume of her unwashed clothes. She really stunk. Daphne shut her eyes tightly.

She knew what was coming... She felt the sticky snot and thinner spit dribble over her mouth, and the doughy fingers beginning the disgusting process, spreading the filthy muck in even swirls across her face. Daphne's skin tingled in humiliated rage, but no outward sign was visible. The fishy lumps of meat probed Daphne's soft and delicate features... then more gunge splattered, separated, and was worked efficiently and with venom into Daphne's lustrous hair...

'Think yer pretty now, little whore? Not much of a Virgin Mary now are yer?'

Ethel was breathing heavily; her frustration and resentment were clear. Rosie intervened... 'Ethel, Ethel... Leave her now, come on we'll be late for tea.'

Ethel sighed, but did leave her now... tea was too

important to be missed for the over-fed trollop. Tomorrow was another day...

Daphne rose nervously... and stood quietly, her slender fingers twisting the hem of her crumpled frock... Ethel eyed her with hatred. 'Still gonna be Mary and cradle the baby Jesus? I don't think so yer little snitch...'

Daphne flinched as Ethel moved close again, threatening... but somehow Daphne uttered one word... calm, assured, albeit whispered. 'Yes.'

Before Ethel could respond, Rosie cut in. 'Oh come on Ethel, Mum'll lash us.' Rosie loathed being late for tea... like Ethel she was always hungry... Suddenly Ethel came to her senses... this could wait.

'Git, yer guttersnipe... Go on... run. Run to yer grubby mum and dad.'

Ethel and Rosie watched Daphne scuttle across the Common, and then turned and made their way along the footpath and up Lamb Lane.

Once out of sight of her persecutors Daphne slowed her pace and whispered to the elm trees as she passed beneath them; they whispered comfortingly back... rustling their browning leaves in the cool evening breeze. Winter was near. Daphne was a pretty girl and Ethel and Rosie really were donkeys. Daphne's troubled mind was briefly happy at that thought, and she broke into a skip, that lasted almost all the way home.

The church clock struck six. Ethel and Rosie gorged their tea, making similar animal noises to their parents; it was a sweaty affair as they slurped, grunted, and sniffed their way through the second course of spotted dick and lumpy custard.

Daphne sat contentedly by a crackling, bright yellow fire; freshly baked bread and homemade plum jam, and a large mug of steaming hot tea lay in the hearth beside her. Mrs Boot ruffled her daughter's hair lovingly...

'How was school...? Oh! Daphne, your hair?!'

'Yes, I'm sorry Mum...'

'But aren't you going to explain?'

Daphne stayed silent... What could she say?

'You're a funny one... Eat up your food; I will wash your hair for you before your father gets in.'

When Zach Boot came into the kitchen he felt the warm glow... his wife and beloved only child sitting at opposite ends of the room. Mother and wife sitting in the solitary armchair, and Daphne in her dad's rocking chair, absorbed in a book... The family Bible. Lizzie Boot looked up and smiled. 'Hello Zach... I'll just get your tea.'

'Thanks luv.' He sat down at the rough table in the centre of the room and opened the newspaper. 'They reckon there'll be snow before too long, Lizzy, and I don't doubt it; we'll have to think about getting some more coal... and Christmas is coming Daff... Daff?!'

'Mmm... yes Dad?'

'Daff, I said Christmas is coming... well soon, we'll be collecting holly, and cutting a tree and buying little presents...'

'Yes I know Dad, and the baby Jesus, born to save, will come again... but this time all over the world, to bring peace and rebirth... There will be no wise men this time though... they will not be needed... it will be a new beginning.'

Her face was radiant, and he noticed for the first time that her cheeks were a little fuller, her body a little firmer... but this did not concern him. After all his daughter was growing into a young woman, seventeen in a few months... but he was puzzled by her reply. Suddenly it occurred to him she was playing Mary in the school play, a first for the senior school, a different take on the Nativity... 'That's right, my little girl is playing Mary in the school play. She'll make a smashing Mary, won't she Lizzie?'

Without looking up from her knitting, his wife agreed. All this talk about Mary and the baby Jesus had made her faintly jumpy. She was forty-two, and pregnant herself... goodness knows how, she had regularly taken her pill and yet here she was... due any day now...

Zach started up on a familiar theme. 'And what will we be calling our own bundle of joy? We still haven't decided...' Zach had asked this question often over the last few months, and so many names had rung merrily round the walls of the stone kitchen but still no decision had been made... Once he had mentioned the name Emmanuel, if it were a boy; Lizzie had thought it was a good choice but Daphne had burst into tears and cried out, 'No! No! We mustn't.'

She had wept inconsolably until her father and mother had promised not to consider the name. Secretly Zach wanted the name John, or Joan if it turned out to be a girl. Lizzie secretly knew it would be a boy and the name they would choose would be

John. It was an incomprehensible feeling. Daphne had mentioned no other name but John when asked. Both parents were puzzled by their once elfin-like child, so beautiful, angelic almost and yet worryingly distant, and prone to extreme emotional outbursts... She was putting on weight too... not a great deal but enough to concern them... she ate so little.

'Daffy...?'

'Yes Dad...' Daphne looked up, and the fire danced in her deep blue eyes. She looked nervously at her dad.

'Daff,' a thought had come to Zach Boot, he was more than intrigued, 'what do you mean when you say the baby Jesus will be born this Christmas all over the world but the wise men won't be there?'

Her lip trembled... she looked at her father with sadness... her eyes brimming...

'It says, Daddy... it says he will come again... and he will this Christmas, but there won't be any wise men... the 'kings' will be too busy this time.'

Lizzie put her knitting down at this and Zach straightened in his chair... he looked cross. 'Has that silly Miss Meadows been putting funny notions in your head again, Daphne?' He looked sternly at her.

'No! Dad!' She looked incredulous.

'Look Daff,' he sighed heavily this time and continued, 'it says in the Bible that when Jesus rose to Heaven two men asked the disciples why they were worrying, and told them Jesus would come again in like manner. Nothing is mentioned about babies or wise men missing... they were there at his birth...

nothing said about kings being too busy... The second coming surely isn't anything about...'

Daphne's face flushed and she showed a rare flash of anger. 'Dad, it will be as I say.' Her lips were firmly pressed together.

'But...' The first gasps of a crying fit stopped her father from going any further. Lizzie saw it coming... the increased breathing and the heaving would be followed by the heart-rending sobbing... Lizzie was scared... Her daughter's behaviour of late seemed to be replicating her own emotional turmoil as her pregnancy progressed... Surely Daphne couldn't be pregnant, oh please God no.

And yet all the signs were there. No, it wasn't possible... was it?

She dismissed these mad thoughts and intervened. 'Now Zach, if the child wants to believe it, what harm is there? Leave her be.' Lizzie's arms encircled Daphne, soothing her; the fit subsided before the first tears but Lizzie was alarmed... Her daughter's body was indeed plumper and her breasts heavier... why had she not noticed? She said nothing... she would, but not now... not now...

Zach grunted and returned to his newspaper... The clock struck eight. 'Time for an early night, my love... Off you go. You are tired... I'll pop up in a while to see you're settled... ok?'

Daphne nodded and rose and left the comfort of the warm room, but lingered long enough on the stairs to hear her father mutter, 'You know Liz, I'm not happy about this play thing; ever since that daft Miss Meadows told her she would be perfect for

Mary, she's been acting odd... almost like she was a bloody pregnant Mary.'

Daphne heard her mother reply, 'Zach, I know, I know, but once the play is over she'll soon forget all this nonsense; me having a kid after all this time hasn't helped; it's affected her, the poor little mite doesn't know whether to be excited or sad.' Mind you, she was hardly a little mite and Lizzie was alarmed at her daughter's possible state...

Daphne trod noiselessly and knowingly to bed... Her mother came up to talk but Daphne pretended to be asleep... In her arms lay the Bible. Her mother left the room, and switched the light off and closed the door quietly. When her mother had gone down the stairs, Daphne crept out of bed, took her nightdress off, and stopped up the crack under the door with it. She then went to the dresser and pulled out a candle and a box of matches.

The candle flickered into life and illuminated the dresser and its long mirror... The naked figure it beheld showed the definite signs of imminent motherhood. 'Baby Jesus,' Daphne murmured and then blew out the candle, returning it to the dresser drawer, along with the box of matches, and then collected her nightdress and put it back on.

*

A few weeks later

By early November the weather had changed and winter had taken an early bite... Late October had been warm but now the bitter winds of mid-November and frosty mornings were the norm. Zach and Lizzie Boot had become increasingly alarmed by the change in their daughter's eating habits... her once slender frame had started to grow quite chubby... She was starting to resemble Ethel and Rosie and always seemed to be hungry... She was worrying them...

Ethel and Rosie, still smarting from being ignored for the school play, had continued taunting Daphne but now had something else to use against her... She was almost as undesirable as them and she was definitely waddling... They were perfectly disgusting in size but Daphne was catching up and they suspected that the 'Virgin Mary' was eating for two and cruelly teased her with a vicious rhyme...

'Jack the Ripper stuck his dirty dipper in her little hole. Ugly baby... grubby lady all covered in coal...'

They knew that in truth she was no larger than them and that their suspicions made no sense and were the product of their nasty minds and fantasies, but it was fun to hurt Daphne in this way... deliciously so... and much less easy to detect or prove than 'beating her up'.

One afternoon in the middle of November, Lizzie Boot went into labour... The village midwife was called and Zach Boot had to virtually drag Nurse Tremlett from her bed to attend to his wife... Two other babes had been delivered in the early hours of the morning and the nurse was exhausted... When Daphne had returned from school in the darkening gloom she had found to her delight that she now had a baby brother. Mother and baby were fine and Zach Boot was to be found sat in the kitchen whistling softly the tune to 'Oh Jonny'. Daphne was certain the boy had been named.

'Dad... is he to be called John?'

'Yes my little dumpling, he is...' He smiled and then hugged his daughter and took her up to see the new baby.

When the house was asleep that night, Daphne stood naked once again before the mirror, bathed in the light of the rude flame, caressing the Saviour in her womb. Daphne was barely seventeen and knew vaguely how babies were made... lessons in school had enlightened her slightly and she had watched the horses in the back field and watched them... seen the female grow large and the foal being born. But the child inside her was not the result of any of that... she had never even been kissed by a boy, let alone... She hadn't even seen a boy's 'dipper' as Ethel and Ruby had so crudely put it...

That was the mystery... and yet she knew she was carrying one of the new children of God... she just knew it.

Ethel and Rosie had given up trying to frighten and bully Daphne out of her leading part in the Nativity. They had realised it was useless... The cruel names and insinuations continued though... but strangely... secretly they had become afraid of her... her intensity and resolve... In fact they tried to avoid her.

*

Elijah Septimus Gudgeon had escaped from Shenley Mental Hospital in March – he had experienced a vision that he was the Holy Spirit, pronouncing the Second Coming of Christ. He had seen Daphne crossing the Common and had instinctively known... the glory of God had filled the air around Daphne. He had danced with the swirling wind... a wild, frenzied dance that had enveloped Daphne, made her feel dizzy and sick and then he was gone... blown inexplicably away by the raging wind and when he had gone, Daphne had felt the strange stirring in her belly. That was the mystery; no 'dipper' had been used... just this awesome swirling wind...

After her brief encounter with Elijah, he had been captured talking to a solitary rabbit; frozen with terror, or rapt with attention, it had remained motionless, staring in wonderment, long after he had been taken away. Daphne had gone home to read her Bible. Then late second term Miss Meadows had selected Daphne for the role of Mary. *Divine intervention*, Daphne had thought... Her Bible had given her the words, her dictionary, the meaning. Daphne had been perplexed.

Daphne was playing opposite a boy called Daniel Divine in the play; it was a sign, Daphne believed. The Bible was full of signs, but no one took much notice these days. Daniel was a boy with very poor eyesight and bullied for that reason, so to be let in on Daphne's secret, her miracle, elevated him, made him feel worthy and protective. He was caught up in her religious rapture; he didn't really understand how she was going to have a baby but he almost believed she would and if she did, it was his duty to protect her.

He went along with her plan, even suggested his father's cellar for the birth; his father owned The Saracen's Head pub; the cellar was partly used for storing coal! The days passed and December was soon upon them. Two days before the Nativity play was due to be performed, on a bitterly cold and particularly frosty evening, Daphne and Daniel disappeared... Their desperate parents searched all night, along with the police and most of the village.

Early the next morning, exhausted and hungry, the search was called off, for an hour, so the throng could get some breakfast and a change of clothes. During the night the weather had worsened; snow had fallen heavily and was now thick on the ground... During the lull in the search the BBC announced its terrible message, whilst the Boots and everyone else warmed themselves by hastily made fires and sipped tea, cradling the mugs in their hands to put life back into their chilled fingertips...

'THIS IS A NUCLEAR ALERT!! THIRTY SECONDS AGO THE UNITED STATES LAUNCHED THEIR FULL ARSENAL OF NUCLEAR CAPACITY... CLAIMING THE WHOLE WORLD WAS HOSTILE... IN RESPONSE RUSSIA, IRAN, THE EEC, ISRAEL, SOUTH AFRICA, CHINA AND NORTH KOREA RECIPROCATED... You are advised to take Civil Defence Action... You have no more than 20 minutes to do so... This is the BBC...'

The broadcast ended and all the radios, televisions and Internet went dead... Phones fell silent... no signals. Moments later, Zach Boot, initially stunned, screamed, 'Into the cellar Liz... quick.' Lizzie scooped up baby John... Her husband grabbed the shopping trolley, normally used for collecting wood, and grabbed the contents of the fridge and pantry and threw as much as he could muster into it. Spoons, knives, and a tin opener clattered in too. His last act before fleeing was to snatch the radio off the kitchen table.

Coal had been delivered the week before and was now piled high at the entrance to the cellar, further down and back there was an empty space. Lizzie sat stupefied; the baby gurgled contentedly... totally unaware. Furiously Zach Boot dropped the trapdoor, and stumbled to his wife's side. Inside the pitch black cellar they heard nothing but the coal ever so gently shifting after being disturbed.

Miss Meadows sat alone in her own coal cellar... praying for a miracle...

Many in the village had not heard the warning, others had been too horrified to move, some had even gone out onto the streets to watch the missiles drop and explode! All perished. Ethel and Rosie had refused to budge from the breakfast table; their last few moments were spent wolfing down eggs, bacon, sausages and numerous slices of fried bread. Anyway... their parents had no coal cellar to retreat to; instead their open fire had been replaced by one of those lovely coal-effect gas fires... it went up a treat when the house was swept away.

Curiously, it has to be noted that by the dusty remains of Ethel and Rosie lay, unspoilt, the costume they were to wear for the Nativity... a late addition to the cast – the donkey...

Many days later Daphne and Daniel emerged from the ruins of the Saracens Head; a grey and wet day. The pair and their charge remained dry... the spirit of Elijah Septimus Gudgeon lived on, swathing them in a blazing, protective halo of light. Within the glory of light Daphne climbed onto a donkey that had suddenly materialised; her bundle was handed up to her. The donkey trod warily but confidently on the broken ground. Daniel led the way, his face shining with innocence and wisdom... the baby Emmanuel slept soundly.

On the other side of the Common Lizzie and Zach emerged from their cellar, joyous to be alive; their baby was, if anything, slightly wild eyed. The grief in their hearts was tempered by an uncanny feeling; devastation surrounded them and yet...

A bright light shone in the distance; far across the Common a similar light beckoned. The Holy Family continued on their journey. Zach and Lizzie watched in awe as the donkey came into view. Daphne climbed down and revealed her baby's face...

'Mother... Father... this is Emmanuel.'

Miss Meadows strode into view... she had been the beckoning light. Together they all ascended into Heaven... On the way they passed the Gates of Hell and glimpsed Ethel and Rosie being force-fed by a pig.

The Earth underwent rejuvenation; the survivors returned... there under the whispering Elms sat Miss Meadows, much younger and very much in love with one Elijah Septimus Gudgeon, no longer deranged... if he ever was... and very much alive.

His youthful looks and bright smile welcomed the dawn of a new Eden...

In every country around the world this strange wondrous scenario was being repeated... In every nation... a baby Emmanuel and a baby John... a new beginning... the Earth cleansed and ready to start again...

7

Justice

Ivy Peake was sixty-three years old, mauve hair, a drooping chin, and enough false teeth to bite you to death. Her tongue was the problem, or to be more precise, the use of it. The chaos she had caused, and was continuing to cause, had led to restraining orders, lawsuits, and complete isolation; even her family had disappeared, and quietly changed their names. Her telephone bill was astronomic; she lived in squalor, and was many months behind with her rent, but her all-consuming passion remained undiminished... undimmed.

Since Billy, her late husband, had flown the nest, so to speak, she had become a veritable nuisance. Billy had expired on top of Miss Deerlove, the local postmistress, a clinch that had made all the more embarrassing because Mabel (Miss Deerlove), had been forced to call for assistance through the open bedroom window, upon realising that she was trapped under Billy's volumes of flab. It was not the climax she envisaged when, some half an hour before, Billy had offered to take a look at her wayward and rusty plumbing!

Unfortunately for her, and the rest of the community, as it turned out, Ivy just happened to be under the window, talking to Mrs. Blunt about unmarried mothers, when Mabel had called out, 'Oh my God! Help, help, help!'

Both women had stopped their conversation and looked up in consternation.

'Please help me. Oh God, oh God, someone please!'

Stan Flick had just emerged from the Blue Anchor public house, off duty, and heard the frantic pleas at about the same time as the two gossiping women. Upon reaching the Post Office he called out, 'Miss Deerlove? Are you all right? Miss Deerlove?'

The answer was hysterical, 'For Christ's sake, get him off me. Oh Stan get him off, I can't breathe.'

Stan had broken the door down, and hurtled up the stairs, closely followed by Ivy Peake and Doll Blunt. What they found, once inside the bedroom, was beyond all three of them. There before them was the limp, very nude, and very sweaty mortal remains of Bill Peake, and crushed underneath him the pert, heaving, struggling form of Mabel Deerlove.

Mrs. Ivy Peak had collapsed in a quivering, moaning, blubbering heap. Doll Blunt had stood, mouth agape, but with a glint of malevolent satisfaction in her one good eye, and Stan Flick had exploded – Miss Deerlove was, after all, his fiancée!

The funeral, intended as a quiet affair, had turned into the event of the year. From beginning to end it was an unmitigated disaster, and only furthered Ivy's resolve to get her revenge on all and sundry. Miss

Mabel Deerlove had fuelled a smouldering fire.

Ivy, bereaved, but furious, had asked for a moderately inexpensive send-off; she had just got that. The local Catholic church, ever mindful that time is money, had incorporated Bill's funeral in the eleven o'clock Mass – Ivy was not aware of this technicality, and as a result was initially bemused at the numbers that had turned up, in all their finery. The priest, Father Donald Larry, was delighted; for the first time in months he had a captive audience.

Billy was already firmly in place, and had been since the previous evening, attended, sadly, by very few flowers, but virtually engulfed by mourning cards of various shapes and sizes.

Ivy was entrenched in the front pew, accompanied by her son and daughter-in-law, her brother, and Doll Blunt.

In the next row back sat the estranged daughter, and her only grandchild, Mountain – her daughter's idea of a joke no doubt!

The church was full of neighbours, 'sympathetic', and otherwise; many faces easily recognisable, some vaguely familiar, others were strangers, but their demeanour suggested some sort of association with Billy. Stan Flack was there in his neatly pressed police uniform; Mabel Deerlove sat a distance away from him, alone, but demure, in a blue chiffon number that showed good measure of her ample attributes – 'a dirty cow' was how Doll Blunt had put it after the shameful discovery.

Father Donald Larry began as if Bill wasn't there, and spent most of the service virtually ignoring the rather shabby box that stared up at the purple-coated alter. The rain lashed down outside, creating a tribal dance effect inside – the incense wafted generously amongst the congregation, invoking much watering of eyes, clearly adding to the 'natural touch'. There was much coming and going for the rapidly imminent Communion. Sidney Plackett, a rather gross altar boy, with exceedingly spotty visage, unexpectedly slipped, bringing second helpings of red wine to the ruddy-complexioned priest, and tumbled the length of the altar steps in his grotesque platform boots. After giving a passable imitation of a clog dancer on his back, and with much squirming and writhing to right himself, he managed to wobble to his feet, and ascend to his allotted place next to the vexed priest. When the guffawing congregation had recovered to giggles, and titters, the service continued rapidly. Throughout, Billy, the deceased, was only mentioned, in passing, three times. There was no eulogy, no platitudes, in fact nothing to suggest it was a funeral at all.

As the coffin was hitched onto the pall-bearers' shoulders, the priest hobbled to Ivy, still in the front pew, and explained in a whispered tone, clearly in agony, 'I've the runs… something chronic… Mrs…' And was gone, shouting, as he bolted through a side door, that he would see them all at the cemetery in twenty minutes, God willing! Ivy turned to see her Billy move swiftly down the central aisle, followed by an impatient congregation. Ivy lingered for a moment, and looked upon the Messiah's face, then as if as an afterthought, hurriedly collected the 'sympathy' cards, and stuffed them into her black shoulder bag. Outside, the rain, torrential, 'washed away the sins of the world'; Ivy marched steadily into it.

The 'family' cars had been laid on to transport the immediate kin – in the event, only one was used by 'family', and then strictly it was not wholly family. In fact the second car in the cortège, behind the hearse, contained Ivy and her one-eyed 'friend', Doll Blunt, and that was it. Malcolm, Ivy's son, had declined occupation of one of these cars, pleading the need for a 'fag'; his wife Lorretta, a beagle if ever there was one, followed Malcolm into their Opel Kadett. The estranged daughter, Polly-Maude, and her son, Mountain, refused point-blank to sit in anything paid for with Peake money, and Hubert, Ivy's rake of a brother, would not be parted from his three-wheeled motor scooter, complete with plastic-coated metal shopping basket, and Honda racing helmet! So, in the second 'family' car were two unknown nieces in outrageous dress, from Bill's side of the family, an odd sallow youth, carrying a mandolin, and some skinny old tart, with polka-dot stockings, a red miniskirt, and a hair lip.

Ivy was beside herself, not with grief but pure, undiluted rage – all those people had witnessed the behaviour of her family.

At the first set of traffic lights the hearse went through amber, and a bus cut up the first 'family' car, a milk float pulled out between the first and second car, and when the lights changed, Hubert's monstrous 'little bike' shot past Ivy's car and the errant bus, and settled down to a leisurely fifteen miles an hour, putt-putting up Brampton High Street.

When the ragged and bedraggled cortège pulled into the cemetery, a howling gale joined the rain, and was proceeding to scatter the pathetic flowers, pall-bearers, and mourners in all directions. By the time they regrouped at the graveside they looked as if they had been out at an all-night orgy!

Doll Blunt failed to pay her last respects to 'the dear departed' on account of the fact she, and her umbrella, were dancing wildly among the headstones some fifty metres away – the silly woman had refused to be parted from her umbrella, and was in effect being carried away like some latter-day Mary Poppins, though somewhat older, and more frumpish.

Ivy hardly had time to blink before the coffin was lowered bumpily into the gaping hole.

'Sorry, must rush, err, Mrs, err… wedding at two, anyway I think I've messed myself, most unfortunate, really, and very uncomfortable I can tell you. Well, bye.'

As the dreadful priest rushed away, Ivy dreamily pictured the headlines in The Sun… 'Holy Man Shits Himself At Funeral'. She very nearly smirked. Suddenly Ivy was shaken into reality by one of the black-clad teenagers, purple lipstick, and toilet chain accessories. One of Bill's nieces, she thought. The black leather jacket, and silvery zipper had planted itself directly in front of Ivy. The black bin-liner vest rustled as the slowly descending zipper revealed crimson roses.

'One each, come on now.'

Ivy, rigid with horror, accepted the single rose proffered and watched in astonishment as the remaining tokens were handed round by the extraordinary-looking girls.

'Frow it in now, Auntie, you're first.'

Ivy almost toppled into the hole as she shuffled blindly to its edge. Thankfully she checked herself just in time, and with dignity, dropped the rose.

The rest of the dripping and forlorn assembly followed suit. The shifty youth with the mandolin looked furtively about, and then seemed to have second thoughts. Ivy was already stumbling away, but she heard the first clods of earth splatter violently onto the coffin. The car door slammed shut, and the vehicle squelched homeward.

Ivy thought, *He's going to play that bloody mandolin!*

A reception committee awaited her, all the 'mourners' who had not braved the journey to the graveside. Ivy was by now in deep shock. Who were all these people? A gabble of voices and jostling sandwich snatchers, slurping tea, greeted her once inside 10 Evadne Terrace. She could take no more, but more was to come as she slumped into a chair.

Above the drone of suitably reverent mumbling, a high-pitched twang penetrated the fog.

"Ello Hen, lovely man, your fella, such a shame I'm going like that.' The face of the skinny tart with the hair lip thrust forward.

'Who are you? Who…?' Ivy was struggling to focus.

'Me, me!? I'm Lill, Lilly Truworf. I knowed your hubby,' there was a sly look, 'intimately, yer might as well know.'

'I beg your pardon?!' Ivy didn't understand, but some vague notion was beginning to alarm her – there were more… more than she thought?

'Ohh eeh wouldn't 'av told yer about me now, would he? The old scallywag; err, 'old on a bit... Loneee, Loneee luv.' The woman's voice carried in the direction of the youth with the mandolin, who had his hand up the skirt of one of the black-clad teenagers.

'Yes Mum?' he said this as he removed his hand. Using the same clammy paw to scoop an egg and tomato quarter into his mouth, he made his way across the room to the waiting, painted mother, and the mourning widow.

'Leoneee, what yer doing? I want you to meet Billy boy's wife.' She knew full well what lecherous Lonny was doing.

Lonny was a sickly youth of about nineteen, long and greasy, with a touch of Bill about the eyes!

'Mrs. Peake – my son. Lonneee; Lonneee tell 'er ow much you're going to miss yer old dad.' The skinny tart sniggered.

'I'm sorry! What did you say? What do you mean?' Ivy's face was flushed.

'Ooooh dear, now ain't that a turn up for the dog's breath. I don't suppose Billy told you about our Lonny either.'

Ivy's body was trembling. 'Lonny, bloody Lonny, what are you talking about? You stupid old cow.' She was on her feet, and her eyes seemed to be pumping in and out; the ugly, wafer-thin, decidedly purple veins twinkled on her bulbous nose.

Lilly Trueworth was not altogether stupid, and stepped back into the protective arms of her Lonny, as she said, 'Lonny is your Bill's son.'

The lunge became dizzy; Malcolm appeared from nowhere to catch his mother before she crashed onto some dainty teacakes one-eyed Dolly had thoughtfully baked (inadvertently the week before).

Ivy, terribly distressed, was taken upstairs; a sedative was administered.

The next morning Ivy woke; her mind was buzzing and the sun filtering through the partially drawn cherry blossom curtains hurt her eyes. Doll Blunt sat, staring, with her one good eye, at the waking Ivy. Ivy saw her immediately, she turned away from the harsh sunlight. She collapsed on the pillow, her shuddering tears were very real.

'Oh Doll…'

Dolly shifted her chair, and held her close.

'Ivy luv… Ivy… Come on now, here's a cup of tea.'

The 'Teasmaid' gurgled its assent.

Ivy drank the scalding tea greedily, and then lay her head to rest on the pillow again. The yellow tobacco-stained ceiling reminded her of Bill – such a dirty man. The silence was broken.

'Ivy… I've got to tell you… your Bill…'

'My Bill?' Ivy muttered sullenly.

'Yes… yes, your Bill! Ivy… he had most of the women in the village; now I've said it… and I'm glad.' She was too.

Ivy's mouth opened, but before she could say anything, Dolly continued, 'And that Lonny's not the only little bastard that's Bill's either.'

'Oh God...' Ivy wished she had died instead of Bill.

Doll was actually enjoying herself, she too had succumbed to the charms of Bill in her former years, that was why she had only one good eye now – he had punched the other out when she threatened to tell Ivy about their affair, after she had fallen for her Frankie. Her husband never knew Frankie wasn't his, and Doll's eye, the missing one, was explained away – a silly accident with a broken milk bottle, flying glass! Her story had never been questioned at the hospital, or by her husband. Under threat of violence all Bill's other women were sworn to secrecy; Doll didn't care, she had lost her cuckold of a husband the previous year to cancer of the bowel.

Doll gleefully listed the 'fallen' women, Bill's conquests, his children; at least the ones she knew of. Doll, however, underestimated Ivy's hatred for her recently deceased, over-sexed spouse, and also had no conception of the wrath about to be unleashed. For years Ivy had refused William Peak his conjugal rights, ever since the birth of Mountain, her estranged daughter's brat; ever since her whore of a daughter had, with malicious relish, informed Ivy that her grandson was Bill's son! Ivy kept quiet, never revealing to Bill the sum of her knowledge; though Bill must have suspected when daughter and mother ceased speaking to one another.

Ivy had also known about Doll and Bill, but not Frankie; an inkling of other affairs, two or three she was sure of, but now, Doll's list, the tart with the hair lip, and her greasy offspring; where did it stop?

What Doll told her the morning after the burial only served to strengthen and deepen Ivy's determination to make the guilty pay for the years of being cheated, abused, obviously laughed at behind her back. Bitterness scathed within, Ivy would get even.

The plan was simple – the systematic destruction of every family in the village, whether guilty of Bill's shadow or not, they would pay.

The wave of divorces, common assaults, and children sliding into local authority care had slowed to a trickle, but the phone bill continued to rise as Mrs. Ivy Peake cast her net farther afield. No stone would be left unturned; those mourning cards had come in handy, criminals never could resist returning to the scene of the crime for one last look, to pay their respects; if there was no proof, then a lie would do, a suggestion, a hint, no matter, so long as they all paid.

'Hello. This is a friend...' On the other end of the line an unsuspecting husband was about to receive some very unwelcome news.

FROM A TORTURED MIND

Poetry Section

1. Beneath Me

Beneath me I see the sun-baked earth,
Above… the vulture circling, no sound,
Heavy storm clouds gathering at the edge of time,
I cannot fathom how I feel, for there is real fear,
A dread so terrible I can sense the fabric tearing,
The rook is poised…
The knight vaguely aware,
Vulnerable, isolated,
Such terrible unhappiness,
Cannot stem the tide,
Suffocation.

Love, need, aspirations,
All so pointless in,
This state of limbo,
Not knowing,
Failing to understand,
Why the terror,
Crept silently in,
Is this what the passing years,
Deliver as the ultimate gift,
Is this how I end my days.

Sleep does not provide respite,
The demons wait patiently,
The Bishop smiles,
A smug and ugly book,
Prayers for the faithful,
Words for the forgotten,
I can remember I shout,
I do know...

And I feel so sad,
So much has gone,
And I cannot change,
The inevitable slipping away,
The dilution,
Disintegration,
Of my life,
The rainbow has been rubbed out,
The polish no longer effective,
I am tired now, invisible tears break through the
mask,
But they are wasted, destructive,
Burning away the last semblance of sweet memory.

2. *Little Sparrow*

The cold, frightened little sparrow sat alone,
The garden blanketed in white lay asleep,
For the garden had been white for a long time,
Time, what was it? The little sparrow was very
cold.

Fear had kept her there, not knowing anyone.
Why was she still alive, with no food for days?
All living things seemed dead, nothing about,
Strange how she thought it was a garden,
After all there were no buildings in front of her.

Being so cold made her think it was winter,
And yet this cold stuff wasn't wet,
Everything was just white, although what was
white?
For the first time she realised somehow that she
would always be,
Always alone, always afraid, always cold,
The little sparrow understood, the world was dead.

3. Somewhere

A clock somewhere CHIMES,
A child somewhere dies,
A newspaper somewhere dies,
A child somewhere is completely misunderstood,
A car somewhere CRASHES
KILLING ALL PASSENGERS,
A friend somewhere BETRAYS
AND DESTROYS YOUR DREAMS,
A dog somewhere is beaten and bleeding,
A friend somewhere is
SCARED AND ALONE,
A life somewhere is finishing, now do we care?
'We care,' say the people.
HOW CAN THEY?
'We care,' say the governments.
HOW CAN WE BELIEVE THEM?

The man with the stumps,
The alcoholic with liver failure,
The family starving,
The smoker with cancer,
The lonely beings of this world,
WOULD THEY SAY WE CARE?
Have a cup of tea and forget (two sugars please).

4. Mr. Something

Scorched earth, dust on wind, bind us together,
Rain cement us, loosen our tongues, create truth,
Waters of the mind flow, burning heart rekindle the
flame,
A fire burns for so long as effort sustains,
A river flows if its natural course lies uninterrupted,
Calling the united world of fools don't deny me this
one request.

Wizened trees still produce golden fruit,
Injured animals still tend their young,
Yet we the chosen ones cannot get the rain to fall,
Silvery trees glistening with red roses give us life,
Do something, someone, whatever you are, save us
from the fearful waste.

'Man I give you precedence, and yet you are lost.'
How can you help those who suffer your problems?
Pain, fear, we are losing, down the spiral,
The music to accompany you, soft and sweet,
Scorched earth seems to have won after all,
My mind burns, my soul is wretched, I know,
Something can save us, why don't you come, Mr.
Something.

5. Sugar Coated Man

Sickness grows among our ranks,
Squalor, filth, and degradation rule supreme,
Emulating our great democracy of faith,
Distance lengthens ever more, the joy and hope
dispelled.

Sugar coated man ascends the pedestal,
Rich and powerful beyond all ultimate desires,
Behind and beneath him lay the tattered ruins,
The shiny marble reflects the sunlight of the money
gods.

Inner feelings of desolation and hopelessness emerge,
The sugar coated man glances furtively over his shoulder,
Arrayed in war paint the democracy advances,
A flashing blade hovers, then plunges, sugar coated
man, deceased.

The palatial splendour and the iron power crumble,
God is good, so the journal tells, but evil surpasses,
Transcending goodness, challenging the fabric of
equality,
Incarnate, yet another sugar coated man treads heavily
on top.

6. Closing Time

The door closed for the last time,
Joe looked to his domain for one final glimpse of
hope,
The plastic fixtures and glaring lights were his
ultimate gasp,
Clawing back the feelings of regret and pain, he died.

The sun shone through the brightly coloured
windows of Joe's mind,
Joe had started his journey into the timeless zone,
The zone of clinking beer glasses and packets of
crisps,
A mindless world, devoid of thought but full of hope,
Love is a secret process and here Joe sleeps, his
dreams for the future complete.

His dull and drear wife, Ethel, brinks on suicide,
But still the endless, comforting cups of tea arrive,
Joe and Ethel walk to the garbage can, hand in grimy
hand,
They climb in, amongst the disposables, their lives
rejuvenated.

7. The Suitcase and the Jew

The escalators rattled happily along, eight thirty going
on nine,

Still in bed, small bedsit down by the river, pleasant,
nice, acceptable,

Monday morning, raining as usual, nice day though,
smile, that's right,

Must get up now, be late, can't do that, never late, oh
well, just once,

Nice and easy does it, carpet cold, bed warm, kittling
boiling, oh well,

Radio on, nice tune that, wishing for a woman, who
though? Never mind.

At work now, lots to do, still nearly lunch, where to
go? Oh well,

Lots of people going to lunch today, down the pub I
think, yes,

Smokey in here, nice though, lovely barmaid, big
breasts, oh yes,

Time up, see her tonight, oh yes, she will come, I'll
have her then,

Cup of tea, a biscuit, take her home, that's nice, all
right,

Underground bustling, that's nice wash hair, have
bath, best suit.

Seven thirty that's right, suitcase standing, good boy,
we'll see,

Down the pub we go, no way stay here, may need you
later,

There she is. 'Hello Jew, hello Jew.' Nice girl, oh yes,

Closing time, come on, that's it, soft skin, silken hair
nice,

Open door, in you go, take your clothes off, oh yes
soon there,

'Jewboy don't want you, dirty, horrid, nasty little Jew.'

Suitcase smiling just the same, cup of tea then, that's
right,

Room dark now, oh yes, put clothes on, oh no you
don't.

Don't scream, that's it, lovely, one more leg, painful,
oh well,

Suitcase getting heavy now, nice, enjoying it now,
nearly done,

Must clean carpet, river flowing, suitcase happy, oh
well...

8. God And The Boy Who Loved Him

'God, creator of the world, how beautiful you are,
How rich and splendid is your Kingdom,
Love me Lord as I love you, oh princely one,
Give me your light and happiness oh God of mine.'

The boy picked his way through the ruins of the city,
A city once as splendid as God's Kingdom,
Now its beauty faded, its squalor revealed,
'Boy why praise your God?' a voice sounded through
acid rain,
The foul stench of rotting, animal flesh wafted,
The emaciated boy's nostrils wrinkled,
He felt very sick, all around, desolation.

'God I understand, we all have to take a holiday,
But why do you take so many?'
God smiled down on the boy and yawned,
He answered the little boy's question readily,
A crumbling building fell on the child of God,
He entered his beloved God's Kingdom of Heaven.

9. *Watchie*

Silently slumbering the watchman, dreamt of money,
muti and the death of the white man,

Ten long years of his life had ambled by, softly he
slept,

How many trees had suffered to keep him warm?
Now there were no more trees.

The white man was still here strutting proudly,
growing richer,

But then so too were fellows, who had once held his
self-same station,

As grey clouds hurried by, he reached into his dreams
and took another shot.

Alcohol had saved his sanity, provided fantasy, but
destroyed his mind,

Painfully he was aware, he was going nowhere, month
end soon,

A harsh voice startled him from his fitful sleep, he
opened his big round eyes.

Through bloodshot haze he beheld the white devil
incarnate,

He stiffened, fear and hatred welled up in his failing
heart,

Now was the time, now, he lunged, the white beast sprawled helplessly,

The great white whale had ten years due to pay,

'Watchie's' foaming mouth signalled the end,

An embittered moan uttered from the developing corpse,

'Black Bastard.' 'Watchie' staggered, he too knew it was over,

The white predator, not so white now, as the dagger shimmered in moonlight,

'Watchie's' body slumped, pain, sadness, but no remorse,

The rain fell heavily, and together they lay side by side,

Death however brought them no closer, the hatred remained.

10. The Sea Urchin

Softly the rain entered my heart,
Pattering and gliding in channels,
My blood accepted its intrusion willingly,
Bubbling and brimming with ecstasy,
Lulled into false security I slept.

Slowly the rain crept into my lungs,
Filling, consuming every niche, every opening,
My breathing became irregular and short,
Gasping and gushing with urgency now, the rain
gurgled,
I slept on, blissfully ignorant of my fate.

Stealthily the rain trickled into my mind,
Intruding, pressurising, my dreams interrupted,
I fought bravely, heroically but no use,
The rain had tricked me, the stream was no more,
The river had grown quietly until its banks had
burst,
Now the sea crashed me against the rocks,
Fragmenting my bones, separating me,
Slowly, oh so slowly I eroded and broke up,
No more was I, the sea was me and I the sea.

11. Grandparents

Soaring, playing mandolin, Grandma flying so high,
Flutes tinkling, tambourine shaking Grandpa,
Polka dot noises dinking in and out, clouds dancing,
Tribal band on magic carpet beating foot-tapping
sound,
Angels piping all aboard the God train, slowly
moving.

Incredible journey beginning and the band plays on,
Choirs of goblins chant through ever growing misty
haze,
And on and on they go calling all spirituals,
Grandma guitar playing, strumming wildly,
convulsions imminent,
Grandpa pounding piano, perspiration globularising,
heart attack possible.

Wind blowing, choirs reaching crescendo,
Drums beating, louder, storm gathering,
Natural order cracking, lightning strike,
Chaos, panic, Grandma playing double bass spelling
doom,
Magic carpet, Grandpa bearing musical gift from
God.

JOHN K. GERAGHTY

A gift, a gift... Whispers the rain, orchestra
proclaiming,
Fear subsiding, no one left, fear awash,
Jigging across the darkened sky the goblins embroider
the new musical score,
Hornbeams twist their way to the sky, Grandpa's
God-given gift accepted,
Giant cabbages enveloped in musical peace, Grandma
munching softly.

The new order, brickwork, crumbling dust, Hello,
Good morning, the slugs doff their caps to music,
Gentle resurrection, washing the earth, purity
beavering,
Clear, cool springs hunt out disease cleansing,
Grandma and Grandpa fall to earth playing a clarinet
duet.

12. The Whispering Trees

'Goodnight...' said the cripple... 'Goodnight,'
whispered the trees,

'There is something you should know my crippled
friend...'

But their words were muffled, lost by the
strengthening breeze,

He begged and pleaded to hear again...

But they were silent... they were trees after all... they
could not speak...

Inky darkness shrouded the mind... for the cripple
was completely blind,

A creeping fog... a peaceful wood... a dulling moon...

The words he thought he had not heard...they were
there, floating in his mind,

'Soon... soon... my lonely friend...' he thought they
said...

'Oh I wish and pray...' the cripple muttered...

The trees bent gently down and took pity and once
again they softly uttered,

'Soon... soon... my poor, dear friend.'

13. The Embers of Youth

The sweet smell of cut grass, growing at dawn, dead
at dusk,

Yet not so dead, despite your horrific assault, live on,
do you?

Savagely you hew me down but I am made to survive,
to multiply.

I survive despite you, from birth to death you decay
and crumble.

On your way you destroy, your young innocence is
suppressed,

But the embers glow in spite of you, the child never
leaves you,

You leave the child to wonder at his universe, to
tinker with the elements.

Dreamy days of summer paddling in pools of
splendid sky blue,

Cobwebs on misty mornings, heavy with dew,
glistening on dawn's golden sun.

Tiddlers sloshing around in milk bottles of sea green,

Peanut butter melting in balmy waves, dripping from
hunks of freshly baked bread.

Throwing rabbit food from ivory towers on market
day and smiling laughter,

All of these things and many more lie hidden from view,

But views are deceptive and the grass grows again.

14. White Carnations

A glimmering fire, small comfort for the
embittered heart,
The old woman huddled by the almost spent
force,
Ashes would remain and within them her
memories lay,
Once happy faces, that smiling, child all gone, save
whispers in the dark.

White carnations in a milk bottle on a memorial to
the dead,
Monument, glorified by the elements, the rain fell,
A fitful sleep, struggling to remember,
Morning came in but a short while,
The rain fell heavily, washing, cleansing,
One stain, however, never came clean,
The inscription fading, the memory dimming,
But the bitterness and hatred would stay,
White carnations oozing blood, bright red.

Printed in Great Britain
by Amazon.co.uk, Ltd.,
Marston Gate.